FAMOUS

A PACE ACADEMY NOVEL

The Pacesetters...can you keep up?

Simone Bryant

FAMOUS

Recycling programs for this product may not exist in your area.

FAMOUS

ISBN-13: 978-0-373-53430-2

www.KimaniTRU.com

Printed in U.S.A.

For my nephew,

Kal El

"Auntie loves the baby...."

Famous

The Pacesetters…can you keep up?

pacesetters

[páyss sètters] (n.):
a group regarded as being leaders in any field and one whom others may emulate (i.e.: pacemakers, innovators, pacers, modernizers, leaders, leading lights, pioneers, trendsetters)

famous
[fáy mess] (adj.):
very well-known and recognized by many people (i.e.: celebrated, legendary or prominent)

the beginning

We were born to be known. From the moment we were born, people have wanted to see us, know us and in some cases be us. We live the kind of lives most kids can only dream about. We are blessed because of our parents' success. We are rich because of their wealth and fame. And we are worshipped because of their fame.

Fame tops wealth at Pace Academy. We run Pace. We are what it is all about. It's our world—for now.

It's time for *our* shine. *Our* fame.

Who's gonna stop us?

Lights. Camera. Action!

one

Starr

October 13@6:24 p.m. | Mood: Blah

Starr Lester was definitely feeling out of sorts as she lounged across her bed and flipped through the latest issue of *Teen Vogue,* turning the pages with her short, manicured nails with silver minx polish. Her mind really wasn't focused on the glossy pages highlighting the latest fashions. She looked up and scanned the spacious bedroom suite, her eyes settling on the view beyond the French doors to the acres of manicured lawn surrounding the mansion in Bernardsville, New Jersey.

For a moment, she understood how incredibly privileged she was and all that rah-rah-rah. She knew that she'd been blessed. How many kids could brag that their bedroom had an adjoining bathroom with a spa tub, a separate river-rock shower with multiple body sprays, heated tile floors in the bathroom, their own private balcony with an outdoor fireplace, a home theater with its own fully stocked snack bar and a custom walk-in closet that looked like a Rodeo Drive boutique?

That didn't include free use of her daddy's black American

Express card *and* a weekly allowance, along with her own staff that included a part-time personal assistant, a maid and a personal trainer who were all just an email, call, text or tweet away. Top it all off with famous godparents and a circle of celeb-kids as friends, and life was pretty sweet.

She closed the magazine, rolled across the bed and walked across the spacious room to her desk. She balanced herself by bracing her knee against the seat of the fuchsia leather Parsons chair as she leaned forward and picked up the rhinestone-covered picture frame sitting beside her iPad. She curved her lip-gloss-covered mouth into a smile at the photo from her birthday party just over a week ago.

Staring back at her in the framed photo were her father, Cole Lester, the multiplatinum R&B singer-turned-owner of TopStarr Records and a dozen other companies, and her mother, Sasha, the R&B superstar diva who gave up her career for her family. Starr lightly stroked their smiling faces with her index finger. Her parents were famous. Their every move was followed by Perez Hilton–like gossip blogs, celebrity news sites and paparazzi. They lived a *fabulous* life, and made sure that she and her four-year-old twin brothers, Malcolm and Martin, had a pretty wonderful life as well.

Her parents had gone *all* out for her party. Plenty of her friends would love, love, love to say that they had had an over-the-top birthday party that cost her father close to a half-million dollars—not including her custom Range Rover that she wasn't even old enough to drive.

Simply fab-u-lous. It was the party of the decade…just what Starr deserved.

Her eyes shifted to the smiling and supermodel posing

friends—her *besties,* Marisol and Dionne. Together they were the Pacesetters, for obvious reasons, since the three of them definitely set the rules at their school, Pace Academy. Age had nothing to do with their power. It was all about fame—and their famous parents.

All of the kids at their private school had rich parents—attorneys, hedge-fund managers, corporate CEOs and the heirs to family fortune. But only a few had *famous* parents—boldface names that filled the headlines, gossip columns and celebrity news.

Marisol's dad was a Major League Baseball superstar and earned even more money and fame off the field than he did on the baseball diamond. Dionne's father was a platinum-selling artist, who dominated the hip-hop charts.

Starr? Her parents were the most famous of them all. That meant Starr was *the* star of Pace Academy.

No one can deny the power of fame—no one.

Releasing a soft sigh, she left her bedroom and walked toward the elevator a short distance from her suite. She rode the elevator to the basement, humming as she turned to study her reflection in the mirrored walls.

She used her fingertip to feather her hair, still loving the way it brought out her high cheekbones and slanted almond-shaped eyes. The chestnut-brown rinse brought out her light caramel complexion. If she kept the chocolate out of her mouth, then her complexion would definitely stay acne-free. The last thing she needed was for her parents—especially her dad—to invite her to some big event and get caught on the red carpet with a mini-mountain on her nose.

Starr rearranged the delicate ruffles of the blue Valentino

silk shirt under a tailored leather Dolce & Gabbana blazer and a pair of skinny jeans in a dark rinse. She was barefoot now but the navy suede booties she had on when she went to school complemented the perfect blend of textures.

The elevator doors opened and Starr stepped out into the private entrance into the recording studio. Like everything her parents did, it was top-of-the-line—from the design of the three large studios to the sound and mixing equipment in each one.

Starr took the hallway leading to the empty lobby and then across the hall leading to the studios. She loved to spend time in the studios and get caught up in the musically creative atmosphere, as her father and his team of hit-making producers continued to deliver so that TopStarr Records remained the best of the best.

Bored, she just thought she'd pass through to see if there were any new Mariahs, Rihannas or Madonnas in the recording studio.

Starr paused at the glass door leading into studio one. She exhaled a deep breath that left a cloudy residue on the glass as she opened the door and walked into the control room. She lightly touched the digital audio workstation before dropping down into one of the leather swivel chairs. She twirled in the chair with her bare feet high in the air.

Boredom was no fun. Duh.

She leaned her head back and looked up at the ceiling. Her eyes widened at the TopStarr Records logo above her head. She smiled. Pretty fantastic having a record company named after you. It was like she had her own record company and maybe one day she would even run it.

Hmmm.

Now that she'd survived her latest adventure—planning and documenting her "Fabulous and Fierce Fashionista Fifteen" party—another challenge might be big-time fun. Seriously. She was feeling that there had to be more for her to do than just lead a fabulous life. Like there was so much more for her than being loved and adored simply because of her parents.

Starr lowered her head and her eyes landed on the microphone inside the vocal booth.

She wanted to live up to her name—her destiny, her time in the celebrity spotlight.

two

Dionne
October 13@8:12 p.m. | Mood: Excited

DIONNE Hunt used a fuzzy-topped glitter pen to circle the photo in the booklet. Her thin gold bracelets lightly clanged against each other as she added a smiley face and an exclamation point for good measure. "Absolutely perfect," she said, with the biggest, cheesiest grin her face could muster as she tore the page from the booklet.

She hopped down from her full-size bed with the booklet in her hand, her sleek and shiny ponytail swinging back and forth in a direction counter to her retro doorknocker earrings. She left her bedroom and made her way down the hall to the kitchen. Using a refrigerator magnet shaped like a bunch of grapes, she stuck the page in the center of the stainless-steel refrigerator door.

"She has to like this house," Dionne said, literally crossing her fingers and her toes, which were clad in pastel-striped knee socks.

Her life was quickly changing every day, and Dionne was just hoping to hang on for the ride and not chip her manicure.

Two years ago she couldn't have imagined them moving out of their two-bedroom apartment in Newark to the picture of the house she'd pinned to the fridge—a three-thousand-square-foot home in South Orange, New Jersey.

But two years ago her father had been Lahron Young and not "Lahron the Don," a hip-hop star whose debut CD *New Era* dropped and went double platinum within a few months.

Life had changed so much since then. She began spending the weekends and holidays at her daddy's luxury apartment in the same Park Avenue building where Diddy used to live. And she transferred from her old middle school to finish the eighth grade at the ultraexclusive and pricey Pace Academy.

Now her moms had *finally* agreed to let her father buy them a house, moving out of the 'hood to a place where life was all good. "Too bad I had to get robbed for her to change her mind," Dionne said to herself, before she grabbed a bottled water from the refrigerator and made her way back to her room.

Now that she had done the house-hunting her mother kept putting off, Dionne was ready to finish her homework. The letter the headmaster had sent home about her delinquent tuition at the start of the school year made Dionne big-time scared that her new-money father was spending way too much and saving even less. Once she'd worked up the nerve to talk to him about it, he'd let her know everything was cool. But the wake-up call—the possibility of her life going back to what it used to be—made her appreciate what she had, especially being able to attend Pace Academy.

She didn't want to think about what life would be like without going to big award shows and traveling in private jets alongside her dad, or always having money in her designer bags, or not being friends with Starr and Marisol.

Dionne picked up her rhinestone-covered Sidekick, using her thumb to slide it open. She tapped away at the keys with her thumbs as she texted Starr.

What u doing?

She set the phone down and looked up at the image on the flat screen on her wall with the sound on mute. A rerun of *Tiny and Toya* was on, but she didn't bother to turn up the volume. She really needed to finish up her English assignment.

Ding.

N studio.

Dionne shook her head. Starr's life was beyond belief. Right now anyone, from Drake to Madonna, could be at her father's studio recording.

Ding.

Recording. :)

That made Dionne's perfectly arched eyebrows furrow as her thumbs went into action.

No way… W/who? For what? Details!!!!

Ding.

LMYBO. Ssssh! Top secret.

"Then why mention it?" Dionne muttered, trying hard not to take Starr's bait.

She wasn't mad at her friend—just annoyed and *soooo* jealous of Starr.

Tossing her phone to the foot of the bed, she used the remote to turn off the flat screen and moved her books closer to her. Her father had paid way too much in tuition for her not to be an "A" student. She wasn't giving him or her moms any reason to take her away from her life at Pace Academy. No reason at all.

By the time she heard her mom's keys in the door, Dionne had just about finished writing her English paper on her laptop.

"Thanks for the help."

"No problem, Miss Hunt."

Dionne's fingers froze in midair above the keyboard at the sound of voices. She climbed off the bed and left the room just as her mother, Risha, walked down the hall and into the kitchen with Hassan Ali behind her carrying grocery bags.

Dionne literally lost her breath. It's the kind of thing that happens when you're completely surprised by a crush. *Ex-crush,* she reminded herself.

Hassan smiled at her and she could have sworn the gleam of his white teeth went *ding.*

"Hey, Dionne. What's up?" he said, before disappearing into the kitchen.

She was speechless. No words could form in her mouth. She just stared.

Hassan Ali was her eighth-grade crush from South 17th Street Elementary School in Newark. His complexion was chocolate. He had a tall athletic frame and a handsome angular face. There was a confident swagger to his walk.

Oooh, I love him, Dionne thought dreamily.

He could have easily been her boyfriend. But like living in Newark, he didn't fit into her new life. So he was on to the next one—some thick chick named Jalisha, whose body made Nikki Minaj look like a dude.

The fact that he had a girl and wasn't a part of her new world didn't stop Dionne's heart from racing and her knees from weakening.

She smoothed the long-sleeved fuchsia-colored tee she wore over a fitted lime-green tee with a jean skirt—a very casual look—over her slender frame, wishing she'd had time for a fresh coat of lip gloss before she'd walked into the kitchen.

Hassan turned and looked down at Dionne. "You're moving?" he asked, pointing over his shoulder to the real estate listing on the fridge.

"As soon as my mom *finally* finds a house," she stressed, leaning over to look past him at her mother. Her mother's two pairs of gold doorknockers earrings lightly clanged against each other as she was putting away groceries.

Risha Hunt was just thirty years old and looked more like an older sister.

When Dionne looked back up at Hassan she didn't miss the look of disappointment on his face. Her heart tugged.

"I'm not moving to South Orange so you can look again, diva," her mother assured her.

Dionne shrugged as she looked up at Hassan. "You gonna miss me or is Jalisha keeping you pretty focused?" she asked, giving him a soft smile as her heart pounded crazily.

Her mother snorted and Dionne could have died on the spot.

"I miss you now," he said, looking down into her eyes.

"Do you, Hassan?" her mother urged.

Note to self, Dionne thought. *Ask Mom to stay outta my bizness.*

"I better get going," Hassan said, lightly touching Dionne's chin before he turned, leaving the soft scent of his cologne to fill the air.

Dionne inhaled deeply. "Bye, Hassan," she said, trying to sound cheerful.

He gave her mom a wave goodbye before he walked down the hall and out the front door of the apartment.

Dionne had to fight the impulse to go chasing after him.

three

Marisol

October 14@6:00 a.m.| Mood: Not sure…

"GOOD *Morning, Marisol. Rise and shine. Strive to be the very best you can be and there's no limit to how far you can go in achieving all of your dreams."*

Marisol Rivera was already lying awake in her bed when the sound of her alarm clock with its daily motivational message went off. She reached over to turn off the clock, feeling way more tired than fabulous. Well, sorta.

Her father, Alex, was the star pitcher for New York's Major League Baseball team. And unfortunately their run at a division title, and consequently the World Series, was completely dunzo. Because her father was a real team player, he celebrated the wins and mourned the team's losses. He always tried to do his very best year in and year out. So in the days after the regular season, he was in a somber mood—borderline depressed.

Marisol had mixed feelings about her father not making the play-offs. She hated that her *padre* was down, but no baseball in the off-season meant he would be home more often. His life as a superstar athlete meant he was always on the go. New York loved its athletes and Alex Rivera was no exception. His looks and charm only upped his celebrity status.

"Unfortunately that also included groupies, too," Marisol muttered, as she climbed out of her bed with its Egyptian-cotton sheets and custom silk coverlet.

She still couldn't believe her father had been cheating with another woman, something she'd discovered during the filming of a documentary about him for ESPN. Luckily all of the fallout hadn't been picked up by the press, but there had been plenty of drama around their house. As much as she loved her father—she was definitely a daddy's girl—it took her a long time to get over her hurt and disappointment. Even though her parents had stuck it out, she couldn't help but wonder if deep down her *madre* wasn't *muy enojado*. (That's major pissed.)

Marisol took her time going through her morning routine, emerging from her bathroom pampered and freshly showered in a terry-cloth white robe. She smiled thinking of how she'd blamed her father's wealth and fame for his indiscretions. She went on a *fabulous* fast—no makeup, special hair products or designer clothes. It drove Starr mad crazy.

It took a serious pep talk with Mrs. Lester for Marisol to discover that it was in her blood to be a fashionista. The clothes, the hair, the makeup? She was just naturally stylish. Simply fab-u-lous!

Marisol sat at her dressing table and flat-ironed her hair until it was shiny and straight before parting it down the middle for the whole Pocahontas look. She was applying eye makeup when the door to her bedroom suite opened and her little brother, Carlos, peeked in. She loved him but the eleven-year-old knew how to get under her skin.

"Knock before you come in, Carlos," she told him, her accent heavy.

He shrugged as he stood at the door already dressed in his charcoal-gray blazer, white shirt and navy pants that made up his school uniform. "Mama's sick," he said, as he began wandering around her spacious room, randomly touching things.

Ew!

Marisol thought about his love of boogers and stood up to guide him by his shoulders to the center of her room where there was not a blessed thing around to contaminate. *"Lo que le pasa?"* she asked before moving over to her walk-in closet.

"She was throwing up."

Marisol froze, her hand poised over a chambray tunic. Oh. Heck. No. *"Madre dios,"* she whispered, biting off the lip gloss she just put on. Thank God it tasted like chocolate.

She walked toward her brother, grabbed him by the collar and dragged him along as she left her room.

"Hey, I'm telling," he hollered, digging his feet.

She stopped and crossed her arms over her chest. "Why do we always have to play these games, Carlos? You won't win," she told him smugly.

Carlos pulled his baseball cap from his back pocket and slid it over his large, round, black curls. "I'm off to school," he said suddenly, before quickly moving past her to run down the stairs.

Marisol laughed as she made her way down the hall to her parents' suite. One of the wooden double doors was open and she peeked into the sitting area of their bedroom. Her mother was still dressed in her silk pajamas, lounging on a chaise watching the morning news program *Buenos Días* on Telemundo. The double doors on the far wall leading to the bedroom were closed.

"La madre de buenos días," she greeted her, as she walked into the room. She bent to kiss her mother's cheek.

Yasmine Rivera smiled brightly at her daughter, tilting her head back. "Good morning, Marisol," she said with a heavy Spanish accent as she picked up the remote to mute the volume on the plasma TV mounted over the fireplace.

Marisol's eyes skimmed her mother's face, thinking, as always, that she was a taller version of Eva Longoria. "Papi's sleeping?"

Her mother nodded, resting her head against the back of the chair.

"Are you okay?"

"Little tired. I think I have the flu," she said.

The flu or the nine-month sickness called pregnancy? Marisol thought, not sure how she would feel about another sibling.

Another Carlos, the "Booger Eating Terror"? Please no. Perhaps a pretty mini-Marisol to groom? Hmm, doable. Definitely doable, she mused.

Pace Academy

The Way I See It!

PSSST!

Posted in *uncategorized* on October 13@10:00 a.m. by thedivaofdish

I spy…a bun in the oven?

Rumors are flying that one of Pace Academy's own is—to quote a Kardashian—*preggers*.

Looks like there's a lot more than education going on in these hallowed halls.

Smooches,
Pace Academy's Diva of Dish

112 comments

four

Starr
October 14@11:14 a.m.| Mood: Motivated

The cafeteria at Pace Academy was buzzing with the latest post by the Diva of Dish—Pace Academy's resident gossip whose identity remained unknown—at least for now.

Starr pushed her new 32-gigabyte iPhone 4 across the table toward Marisol and Dionne. She arched an eyebrow as she tapped the screen with a slender index finger. "You know who the Diva of Dumb is talking about. We *all* know."

Dionne wiped her fingers with a napkin before she picked up the cell phone and read the latest post. She shared a long look with Starr and Marisol, who was working her way through a fresh fruit salad.

"Humph." Starr couldn't forget the sight of Heather Farmer—stepdaughter of a famous actress and a video-vixen-in-training—throwing up last week.

She didn't miss the look of pity her friends gave her or at least it seemed that way. If Heather was pregnant there was a good chance that Jordan Jackson was about to become her baby daddy. Starr gripped the table, almost digging her nails into the wood to keep from screaming.

Jordan Jackson was the boy she'd been crushing on forever.

And he was also the reason she'd passed out onstage at her party last week—a memory she tried to suppress most of the time. One innocent kiss behind her ear and she was laid out like a beached whale.

But now? She was done-dada. Crush? Completely crushed.

"This is so seriously not gossip-worthy. It's sad, right?" Dionne asked. "Signing with your dad's label and all, he might've messed his whole life up."

And mine, Starr thought to herself. Seeing all of her plans with Jordan—the JorStarr of it all—fade to black. She certainly wasn't crazy enough to want to have Jordan's baby, and she was *waaaay* too young to deal with baby mama drama.

Starr sighed.

"You okay, Starr?" Marisol asked, offering her a chunky piece of pineapple skewered on the end of her salad fork.

Starr smiled as she took the pineapple chunk and then waved her hand dismissively. "I'm fine. I don't have time for Jordan Jackson and for sure he doesn't have time for me."

"Exactly," Dionne and Marisol agreed, nodding their heads as they looked at her with pound-puppy eyes.

"Plus I have another project for us to work on," Starr continued, desperately wanting to change the subject. She crossed her legs and gently tugged at the black leggings she wore with over-the-knee boots.

Dionne looked up from the grilled chicken she was slicing. "Like what?"

"I'm still working out the details, but after school ride with me to my house." Starr was excited just thinking about her plans. All she had to do was work out the details and make it happen. Her spiritualist, Kentu, said, "If you can see it, then you can be it!"

Dionne shook her head. "I can't. I have to meet my moms right after school, but you can fill me in later on Skype," she said apologetically.

Starr eyed her. "Are you staying at your dad's this weekend?" she asked, as she picked up her vibrating cell phone.

"Yes, thank God."

Starr frowned at the text from an unfamiliar number. She used her fingernail to open the text.

Hi Starr. What r u doing?

Her thumbs flew across the on-screen keyboard.

Who is this?

Bzzz.

Natalee. :) We met @ ur house. Remember? Wanna hang out after school?

Starr sighed and put her phone down on the table.

"Who's that?" Marisol asked, biting an apple slice.

"This girl my parents want me to be friends with but

that's a done-dada," she said, sounding bored. "Play dates are *so* first grade. Seriously."

Marisol and Dionne laughed as Starr played with the soft hairs on the back of her head and looked around the cafeteria. She eyed everyone—the jocks, the geeks, the drama kids and the glam girls: both the blonde Kristin Cavallari types and the dark-haired Kardashian wannabes.

"Getting rid of the uniform has its ups and downs," Starr said as a girl walked by in a colorful outfit that she was sure a clown would refuse to wear.

"Alaina." Starr reached out and lightly touched her cinnamon-brown hand.

She turned with a bright smile. "Hi, Starr," she said, sounding like someone from the cast of *The Hills*. Maybe she'd spent time in Southern California because of her father's huge law practice, which had offices on both coasts.

"Listen, there's a thin line between *boho* chic and *hobo* freak," Starr advised her.

Marisol's and Dionne's mouths fell open.

Alaina looked slightly offended.

"Lose the blazer, find flats that match your hose, burn that scarf immediately. And return the belt to the wrestler you stole it from," Starr said, pointing out each offense with her slender finger.

"Uhm, thanks, thanks, Starr," Alaina said, still adjusting her clothes as she stumbled away.

"So anyway," Starr said, pushing away the personal pan pizza that she'd hardly touched. "I can't wait for Friday. I should have everything tweaked out by then."

Marisol and Dionne stared at her.

"What?" Starr asked.

Dionne and Marisol looked at each other and just shook their heads.

"Plus we can finish opening all my birthday gifts," Starr said, her eyes back to perusing the large cafeteria that looked more like a stylish restaurant than a school lunchroom. But then *nothing* about Pace was like other schools.

"You're not done opening your gifts yet?" Dionne asked, wrapping her hair behind her ear to show off a two-carat diamond stud.

Starr shook her head. "I'm going to go through them and give some stuff to charity."

"Bet that won't make it onto the blog," Marisol snapped.

Starr's eyes flashed. "Soon there won't even be a blog," she announced.

five

Dionne

October 14@5:05 p.m. | Mood: Excited

DIONNE was filled with so much energy that she could hardly sit still in the backseat of the real estate agent's Mercedes. She had her rhinestone-covered Sidekick clutched tightly in her hand. "Daddy wants me to text him pictures," she said, leaning her head on her mother's shoulder before she did a little dance tapping her feet on the floor mat of the car.

Risha playfully pushed her shoulder away. "Oh, really? And where exactly is 'Lahron the Don'?" she said sarcastically.

"I don't know," Dionne admitted, sitting up to pull her bone-straight hair from behind her back before she flicked her phone open to text him.

Daddy where r u?

Her Usher ringtone sounded just seconds later.

In the studio making hits to pay for that house!!!

Dionne laughed as she looked down at the screen and texted away.

Make that $$$. Don't let it make u. LOL.

"He's at the studio," Dionne said to her mother, closing her phone and sliding it in the inside pocket of her new navy python Gucci tote.

"The way he spoils you he better stay in the studio," Risha said, eyeing the tote.

Dionne said nothing as she pouted her glossy lips a bit and looked out the car window. She hadn't asked for the bag. Her father had surprised her with it last weekend when she'd stayed with him.

Lord, please don't let her get on that whole "don't build your lifestyle around your daddy's money. It can be gone just as quickly as it came," she thought.

Dionne sighed as the Realtor slowed down and turned right onto a street that sloped like a dip in a roller coaster ride. "You like it, Ma?" she said, her voice hopeful.

Her father was buying the house and it was going to be put in a trust in Dionne's name until she turned twenty-one. But the decision was completely up to her mom, Risha Hunt, who was young but very independent.

Dionne's parents had dated for three months when they were just sixteen. Their relationship had ended way before Dionne was born and oftentimes things were heated between them. Risha accepted no money or gifts from Lahron. She worked at the university hospital and paid her own bills. Her only stipulation was that Lahron take care of his daughter's needs. Her mother would no doubt try to pay her father rent. Dionne shook her head. *My mama don't play.*

"It's a lot different from 16th Avenue," Risha said softly, biting the side of her acrylic tips.

Good, Dionne thought, as she gazed out the window. The houses were huge—although they were still small compared to the sprawling mansions Starr and Marisol lived in—but a million miles from their two-bedroom apartment.

"The school system is first-rate," the real estate agent, Cecily, said, as she turned down a long paved driveway.

Dionne's eyes widened. "No, no. I'm already in another school," she said, shaking her head.

The Realtor looked at her with doubting eyes in the rearview mirror. "The South Orange-Maplewood School District is one of the best in the entire state," she said smugly.

Dionne locked eyes with the woman. "I attend Pace Academy," she said, a little too self-satisfied with a "so there" look when her mother wasn't looking.

Cecily's entire expression changed.

Humph.

"Wow, it's really nice," her mother admitted.

Dionne leaned forward to look through the windshield. "I loooove it," she said excitedly.

Risha laughed and waved her hand. "You said that about the last two houses, DiDi."

As soon as the car pulled to a stop Dionne hopped out and took pictures of it. She barely heard the Realtor explaining all the details to her mom as they walked through the house. She was too excited.

The large kitchen with a huge marble countertop island that was simply perfect for her and her friends to eat breakfast. There was a patio paved in limestone where they could lounge and sip daiquiris—nonalcoholic of course. A nice-size pool where she envisioned plenty of parties that she could invite anyone she wanted to! *Love it,* she thought as they walked through the sunken living with a huge stone fireplace and a wall above it for a flat-screen television.

"If we get a big high-def projection screen we can make this like a mini movie theater," Dionne said, raising her T-Mobile to snap a picture and adding to her growing to-do list of decorating.

Her mom just walked around the empty space and touched things.

"I actually know someone who can install the movie theater chairs and digital surround system," Cecily said, aligning herself with Dionne, who seemed more enthusiastic than her mother.

"E-xact-ly," Dionne stressed, tapping away on her phone as they moved through another entryway into a hall that circled back to the kitchen, leading to a stairway with wrought-iron spindles that led to the second level.

Dionne forgot Starr's advice about staying composed at all times and took the stairs two a time. The upper level opened onto a huge, spacious loft that overlooked the living room on one side and the den on the other. She looked up with her mouth gaped open at the incredible skylight. *In love,* she thought as she opened her arms wide and twirled around with a huge smile on her face.

"Girl, sit down," her mom joked, moving past her to

follow Cecily through the wide double doors at one end of the loft area.

Cecily cleared her throat as she looked at them over her thin shoulder. "Be prepared to gasp," she warned, before she opened both doors wide and stepped back.

Dionne and Risha stepped forward, and gasp they did.

The room was spacious with a fireplace against the far wall and patio doors leading to a small balcony overlooking the rear of the property. Built-in mahogany floor-to-ceiling bookshelves flanked the fireplace. There was a fifteen-foot trey ceiling with a bronze lighting fixture big enough to collar an elephant.

"Oh, that's not all, ladies," Cecily said, with a sense of satisfaction as she stood behind them.

"O-M-G!" Dionne sighed, grabbing her mother's hands to pull her toward the closet double doors.

They opened the closet doors to reveal a twenty-by-twenty-foot room with a dressing area complete with custom shelving, a wall of shoe racks and a large, framed mirror. On the other side off the well-organized dressing area was the door to the master bathroom.

Dionne snapped away with her camera. "Can you imagine taking a bath in that, Ma? Can I use it sometimes?" she asked, stepping inside the tub to stretch out.

"Can *I* use it sometimes? If we get this one it would be *your* house and *your* room," Risha said nonchalantly.

Dionne's eyes popped open.

"*Her* house?" Cecily asked, crossing her thin arms over her chest as she looked beyond baffled.

Risha eyed the red-haired Realtor as if to say, "Mind your

business," before she continued inspecting the bathroom outfitted in warm, neutral earth tones.

"Really, Ma?" she asked, nearly slipping in the spa tub as she scramble to climb out of it and rush over to give her mother a big bear hug.

Life is S-W-E-E-T!

Dionne almost did the old-school running-man dance as she left the bathroom to circle the dressing area. "I can fit all my clothes and my shoes in here. And can we get a big comfy stool for me to sit on to get dressed?" she asked, her heart beating a mile a minute and feeling like she would pass out at any moment.

She walked back into the bedroom. "Ohmygod! I can *finally* have the best sleepovers. Me, Starr and Marisol can even sleep in front of the fireplace."

"Finally?" Risha said pointedly, when she walked past Dionne to follow a chatty Cecily out of the room.

Dionne grimaced and bit her bottom lip. Nothing with her mom was ever *that* simple. She felt the kind of bubble she got in her stomach just before a big test. Risha Hunt was not done with Dionne's *finally.* No dang doubt.

She closed her eyes tightly and crossed everything she could: fingers, toes and tongue. *Please, Lord. Please. I can't take another speech. Please let her let this one go. Give me a pass, Lord. Pleeeaaasse!*

They toured the rest of the house, and Dionne didn't say another word. She wasn't new to this. Risha Hunt was just *waiting* for a reason to, figuratively, grab the mic and deliver a speech.

As they toured the other three bedrooms—one, a mini-version of the master suite—she kept on praying. *Hard.*

"I have one other house to show you not too far from here," Cecily said, opening the rear door for them before she walked around to the driver's seat.

And Dionne was still praying as they climbed into the backseat.

"If you wanted to have your friends over—that I've never met, by the way—you could have done that at our apartment. That is if you're not ashamed of it," her mother said in a low voice just as Cecily opened the driver-side door and slid into the seat.

Dionne slumped down in the backseat, wishing she could disappear.

SIX

Marisol
October 15@2:23 p.m. | Mood: Excited

Marisol looked determined as she removed the ruffled black velour tracksuit she wore walking around backstage in the school auditorium. She rotated her neck and head in a clockwise direction, loosening up as she stretched her limbs. Under the tracksuit was the black unitard she was required to wear, along with pointe shoes, for dance class. Marisol owned a couple dozen of the unitards because of the wear and tear from constant washing and because she took classes two or three times a week.

She eyed herself in the wall of mirrors. *This is all about you, Marisol. Stay in the moment. See it. Be it,* she thought.

She stood on the tip of her toes, *en pointe,* and raised her arms gracefully above her head. Her unruly, curly hair had been tamed into a tight topknot. Even though her rounded hips and ample butt were considered heavy compared to more slender ballerinas, Marisol's form was perfect. She looked like a beautiful, brown, Latina ballerina atop a music box.

When she did her ballet poses, it was calming and relaxing

to her like yoga. She could stay that way forever, lost in her love for dance.

Marisol breathed in deeply then lowered herself to a plié, then turned toward the mirrors to be sure there were no signs of sunken treasure in the back (ew!) or a camel toe in the front (double ew!).

"Marisol Ri-ve-ra!"

She took a deep breath to settle her nervous energy and tried not to let the way her dance instructor, Ms. Pulaski, pronounced her name irk her big-time. Her name was Rivera. Not Ri-ve-RAH!

The way Ms. P's breath kicked liked a mule, Marisol thought her name should be pronounced POO-la-ski.

Setting aside the issue of mispronouncing her name, Marisol eased in between her fellow dance students and quickly took her place. She certainly did not want to hear her name called again.

"Good luck, Marisol," Ms. Poo-la-ski said from somewhere in the total darkness of the auditorium surrounding the stage.

Luck? *Nada*.

Skill? Definitely.

Naturally talented? No question.

This solo was one test she knew she was going to ace, big-time.

Marisol took her pose as the first notes of "Famous" by Trey Songz filled the air. (Side note: Marisol was confident that when she turned eighteen, *she* would be Mrs. Tremaine Aldon Neverson!)

"Acting up in Prada. Spend a couple dollars. Head over to Louis. Do you like Gucci?"

The slow melody with an up-tempo bass line was ideal music for Marisol, combining her formal training in ballet, the heat and rhythm of hip-hop and the sass of salsa. She took total control of the stage with the intricate steps she choreographed herself.

"I can make you famous...famous..."

She smiled softly and bit her lips. *Yes, Trey, make me famous,* she thought. *Yeessss!*

The two-minute routine flew by and when she ended the dance with a series of turns before she slid into a split as the music faded out, she still wasn't ready for it to end.

Marisol loved, loved, loved to dance.

There was a sudden applause, loud whispers and whistles from the back of the auditorium. Marisol quickly climbed to her feet as the stage filled with curious onlookers.

"Who is that? Who is that!" Ms. Poo-la-ski roared like she was ready to charge! "Turn on the lights *immediately.*"

Suddenly the lights from the hallway flooded the auditorium as one of the back doors was pushed open and the culprits rushed out, their stampeding feet echoing as they ran down the hall.

Okay? Seriously. Ew. Boys can be so dang-on creepy, she thought, frowning in aggravation.

"Settle down, ladies!"

Marisol eyed Mrs. Poo-la-ski waving her arms in a crazy flurry of long silky scarves and a paisley-patterned dress that had Marisol wondering about her dance instructor's taste and if she was color-blind.

"Okay, good job, Marisol," she said, reclaiming her seat and motioning for the house lights to be lowered again.

Marisol curtsied as Ms. Poo-la-ski required before she exited the stage.

"Erica Manning."

Marisol shook her head and grabbed one of the hand towels and a small box of trendy Vita Coco coconut water from a cart just offstage. She took a drink of the beverage, which was made from the juice of green coconuts, as she watched blond-haired Erica—with her tall, slender-as-a-pencil and graceful-as-a-swan figure—glide past her.

"Marisol," Erica said, in a way-too-strong Southern accent for having left the South almost ten years ago. In the words of NFL wide receiver OchoCinco: "Chile please."

"Erica," she said with a nod.

The air between them was cool. No hate. No drama. But no love lost either. Marisol just didn't care that Erica looked down on her more rhythmic dancing. As she walked away from the stage, the strains of Beethoven's gazillionth symphony began to play. *Bor-ring. Whateva.*

Erica could do ballet until she bored a hole in her pointe shoes. Marisol wanted to do it *all*. She was fine and fabulous about being more Alvin Ailey than Bolshoi Ballet.

"Good job."

"Girl, you worked it."

"Erica can't touch you."

Marisol smiled at all her well-wishes before she picked up her tracksuit from the floor where she'd tossed it on top of her book bag. She had just zipped up her jacket when her cell phone vibrated in her pocket. She pulled it out, not recognizing the number that sent her a text. She scrolled with her crimson-painted nails to open it.

Cooley's. After school. The butterscotch table.

Cooley's was *the* hangout spot for Pace Academy students and any teens in the area. The exterior was in the shape of a huge ice-cream cone and that, plus its all-white decor, latest music and servers on roller skates, made it a popular spot for teens, regardless of cliques.

Marisol walked away from the chatter and dancing of the rest of the dancers backstage to dial the number back. It just rang for a while and went straight to voice mail. She tried it again.

The cell phone automatically went to voice mail, offering no clues as to who the text came from. *Meet at Cooley's? For what? With whom?*

She texted a reply.

Who is this? Do I know you? Hellooo?

Marisol paced a little in an imaginary two-foot square as she waited for a response. And waited. And waited some more. Erica had sashayed off the stage, and the bell signaling the end of the period let out a shrill alarm.

Bzzz.

The vibration surprised her and she almost dropped her phone, juggling it between her hands. She caught it just inches before it fell to the ground.

Better question—how did I get ur # since u wouldn't give it 2 me?

Marisol checked her Rolex as she hurried from the auditorium. "How did I get your number since you wouldn't give it to me?" she repeated.

It was definitely a boy. Definitely.

But which one?

As she made her way to her locker, she tried to figure out who it could be. She wasn't vain, but plenty of boys had tried to get her number and that wasn't counting the ones crushing from afar.

Dionne was at her locker, stacking her Gucci book bag with books. "Hey, Marisol," she said, tossing her ponytail behind her shoulder as she bent down to zip her bag.

"Whaddup," Marisol said, her mind on the text as she opened her locker. She didn't even notice the shirtless poster of Trey hanging on the inside of the locker door.

"What's up with you?" Dionne asked, standing up straight and smoothing the silk sweater she wore under the charcoal-gray blazer.

Marisol showed Dionne the text on her cell.

Dionne's slender cinnamon-brown face went from curious to teasing. "Another crush, Marisol?" she asked, handing her back the cell phone with a tilt of her head.

Sometimes having so much swag and being so popular scared a lot of boys off, and stopped them from even trying to approach anyone in their clique. Being a Pacesetter could be pretty lonely, even if you wanted a boyfriend.

"Do you remember me telling y'all about some dude asking for my number recently?" Marisol asked.

"Just Percy," Dionne reminded her, with a wiggle of her eyebrows as she held up three fingers that she wiggled as well.

Ah. Yes. Number three on their personal, private and so exclusive list of the hottest boys at Pace Academy. Percy "Good to the Last Drop" Gambling. He most definitely deserved to be ranked in the Top 5. Ow!

"Hmm." Marisol considered the possibilities as she visualized all six feet two inches of total cuteness that was Percy Gambling.

She remembered the day he tried to get her number, but she was still big-time pissed to find out her crush, Corey, had a girlfriend and was playing the field. Percy took the hit for Corey's doggish ways…then.

Now?

Marisol shrugged. Now, she ready for a little fun in her life. She was ready to have a "There Goes My Baby" ringtone.

Can't meet 2day. 2morrow?

She hit Send.

That gave her all night to pick out the cutest outfit to get some serious flirting on…once she had showered and was looking fabulous—not dance funky.

"Can I just call you tonight?"

Marisol's eyes widened at the sound of the deep voice behind her.

"Hiiii, Per-cy," Dionne said sweetly in a little sing-song way as she closed her locker, hitched her satchel on her shoulder and walked away with a wink at Marisol. "Byyyee, Ma-ri-sol."

Life is so unfair, she thought, wishing she was on point.

"Marisol?" he said, coming around to stand in front of her.

She turned, giving him her back. "Yeah, call me. That's cool."

Percy laughed and came around her again, this time reaching out to lightly grab her shoulders. "My breath stink or sum'n? I'm chewing gum. What's up, lovely?" he joked, his East Coast accent just doing big things for her.

"Oh, *madre dios,*" she sighed, pressing the side of her hand against her forehead to hide her face. "I just came from dance class and I'm not feeling very cute right now. You know what I'm saying?"

"There's not a girl in this school who can touch you, and lip gloss and all that makeup crap won't change that," he said, chewing away at his gum.

Her eyes took in his one dimple appearing and disappearing as he chewed.

"Cooley's, huh?" she asked, thinking the movement of his dimple mirrored her heartbeat.

Percy nodded. "Most def."

"Why not?"

seven

Starr

October 16@7:23 p.m.| Mood: Excited

Starr kept checking the time on her iPhone 4 as they lounged on her balcony. There was just the slightest bite of chill in the air and Starr had one of the house staff come in to light the outdoor fireplace and bring blankets to cover their legs as they sat on cushioned chairs. Their snacks and oversize cups of hot chocolate came next. She was nearly bursting with excitement about the announcement she was going to make to the girls. But first she was waiting on a package from her part-time personal assistant, Olivia.

Starr never did anything in a simple way. Never.

"There goes my baby..."

Her eyes shot over to Marisol as she rushed to pick up her cell phone and silence the Usher ringtone that was the official signal for calls between a Pacesetter and her boo. Starr reached for her cup of hot chocolate filled with mini-marshmallows and topped with whipped cream. "Something you want to tell us, Marisol?"

Marisol shifted her eyes away from her phone, her cheeks

visibly blushing despite her light brown complexion. She smiled as her thumbs flew over the keyboard.

"Tell Percy the Pacesetters said hello," Dionne said sweetly.

"'Kay," Marisol said, barely looking up.

Starr froze in surprise but recovered quickly.

Percy? Percy Gambling? What am I missing? And why does Dionne know before me? Say what? Say who?

"I thought you didn't give Percy your number?" Starr said, trying her best to sound blasé, like whateva.

Marisol set her cell phone down on the teak side table next to her chair. "He got it from somewhere."

"How was Cooley's?" Dionne asked, reaching for an oversize marshmallow to stick on the end of one of the skewers on the tray.

Cooley's? Percy and Marisol? A date? Even a pseudo-date? What the hello and goodbye is going on? Starr thought.

"It was okay. We shared a banana split, got our flirt on. Nothing major," Marisol said nonchalantly.

"Aww," Dionne sighed as she stuck her skewer into the fire.

"When was this?" Starr asked before taking a sip of her hot chocolate as the flames of the fire reflected in her eyes.

"There goes my baby..."

"Yesterday." Marisol snatched up her phone.

Humph. "After school?" Starr asked, shifting her eyes to watch Dionne drop the gooey marshmallow into her open mouth.

"Yup. Right after."

Hmmm. Starr had left right after school to get her plans together, so she missed the love connection. "Don't you have dance last period on Thursdays?" she asked. "Please tell me you did not wear that coodie-mama-hugging, butt-molesting unitard to Cooley's?"

Dionne choked on her marshmallow as she laughed.

"There goes my baby..."

"No! I had my tracksuit over it," Marisol said, obviously distracted as she read her incoming text and fired away a reply. "Plus Percy said even without makeup I'm the ish."

Starr rolled her eyes.

"Plus, guess who was at Cooley's eating a huge Jay-Z burger with a Madonna milkshake?"

"Not our resident mama-to-be?" Starr asked, ignoring the emotional gut punch she felt at losing Jordan before she even had him. *Boys. Ugh.*

"I'm just saying old girl definitely looked like she could be eating for two." Marisol threw up her hands like *so there.*

"Oh. My. God. What if Heather is really pregnant?" Dionne asked, this time pressing her melted marshmallow between two chocolate-coated cinnamon sugar cookies. "Can you imagine some girl walking around Pace with a big belly!"

Starr held up her hands and then pointed her ebony-painted nails to the left several times like she was directing traffic. "She got to go. Seriously. It's Pace Academy, not *Baby High,*" she drawled in withering tones, referring to the MTV show about a school just for teen mothers.

"You don't really believe there's never been a student at

Pace that has gotten pregnant?" Dionne asked, looking at them as if they couldn't be that naive.

Starr shrugged. "There've been rumors, but a full-blown my-water-is-about-to-break-in-the hall-at-any-moment pregnancy, no."

"There goes my baby..."

Marisol nodded in agreement before giving in to a sudden text addiction that Starr thought a solid pimp-slap to the cheek would solve.

"You still haven't talked to Jordan?" Dionne asked, chewing on a mouthful of s'mores.

"For what? Obviously he is moving in a faster lane than I want to be in. Jordan needs to continue dealing with the Heathers of the world, because this Starr is too far up there for him to reach."

"Alright now," Dionne said like she was in church saying amen to the preacher in the pulpit.

Heather's fifteen-dollar-an-hour-earning father marrying a famous actress pulling in nearly fifteen million per movie had brought the girl into a whole new world. Unfortunately, she overdid it trying to fit in.

Style? Too sexy.

Clothes? Too tight.

Friends? Too slutty.

Boys? Too needy.

Enthusiasm? Too much.

Legs? Too open.

Ew!

Bzzz. Starr picked up her iPhone. She had a Twitter update. She had over five thousand followers—some of them celeb bloggers and entertainment e-zines. Not bad for a freshman in high school without her own claim to fame. *At least not yet,* she thought.

Her idol and unknowing mentor, Kimora Lee "Oh So Fabulous" Simmons (or Hounsou?) had sent an update. Besides, her friend Kimora was the *only* celebrity she followed other than her parents. Starr simply loved her and knew if she ever got the chance to get within a foot of Kimora, she would drink from her overflowing cup of how-to-be-so-daggone *fabulous.*

@OfficialKimora: Happy Fabulosity Friday!!! To all my fabs! Sending you my love!

Starr looked over her shoulder and through the open French doors as the doorbell to her suite rang. She decided not to use the oversize remote control pad to switch on her plasma television to the channel linked to the security camera outside her door. *My package!* she thought, hopping up from the chaise longue in her Bedhead cotton sateen pajamas that she adored so much that she made sure to keep new ones on hand for her overnight guest. *(What's fab for the host is fab for the guest!)*

Starr rushed to the door and opened it. Sure enough, Mimi, the Lesters' live-in maid, stood there holding a box in her hands. Starr snatched it and stepped back to slam the door closed before Mimi could even say, "You have a package."

Starr was halfway across the room before she turned and rushed back to open the door. She stuck her head into the ornately decorated hall. "Sorry, Mimi. Thank you," she said, breathless with excitement.

Mimi looked over her thin shoulder in her all-black uniform. She just smiled.

All was forgiven.

With her parents being such a power couple in the entertainment industry they were often away at parties, premieres and other events. On those nights, it was Mimi who kept Starr and her twin brothers company during meals.

Rushing to her bed, Starr set the FedEx box down and tore it open, not caring if she chipped the glossy polish on her freshly manicured nails.

"What's that, Starr?" Marisol called from the balcony through the open door.

"Our destiny," she called back, picking up the portfolio folders. "Meet me in the theater room in five minutes."

"Yours or the one downstairs?" Dionne asked.

"Mine," Starr said over her shoulder as she picked up the box and made her way across the bedroom to the double doors leading to her own mini movie theater.

Starr flipped on one of the switches and the room was completely illuminated. She dropped down to the plush fuchsia carpet, sitting down on the huge gold star—like the Hollywood Walk of Fame—with her name in the center.

By the time Marisol and Dionne sat down in one of the soft leather recliners arranged in a semi-circle around the screening room, Starr was standing in front of the curtain-covered wall with a remote in her hand.

"The Pacesetters are going to be famous."

Dionne and Marisol exchanged a brief look. "Huh?" they both said.

"We're forming a group and going to put out a banging CD on my dad's label," she said with the utmost confidence, before walking across the carpet to the concession stand at the back of the room.

"What?" Dionne and Marisol exclaimed, turning in their chairs to study her.

Starr stood in front of the glass counter with all her favorite treats from a traditional movie theater—everything from Goobers to hot dogs. That morning she'd told Mimi that she was having overnight guests and Starr knew everything would be ready for yet another fun and fabulous sleepover at Starr Lester's. Plenty of girls at school would give their Pradas for an invite. But this was just for the Pacesetters. It was their time to talk about the essentials: boys, fashion, gossip…and their soon-to-be claim to fame.

Starr smiled as she pushed a button on the remote. The lights dimmed and the pale gold curtains slid open.

Dionne and Marisol leaned back as the one-hundred-and-twenty-inch HD projection screen clicked on.

"When did you get this?" Dionne asked, squinting as their entire bodies were illuminated by the reflection from the TV. "What is it, three hundred inches? Jeez."

"Focus, ladies," Starr said, ignoring the fact that her parents had upgraded her sixty-five-inch flat screen. "Meet the team that I have hand-picked to help us on our way to destiny."

On-screen was the smiling face of woman in her mid-twenties.

"There goes my baby..."

"Marisol!" Starr snapped in aggravation from the rear of the room.

"Sorry."

After silently counting to ten, Starr continued with her presentation.

"This is Indria, one of the top image specialists in the country. She has styled everyone from Usher to Christina Aguilera."

Click.

"Makeup diva and hairstylist phenom, Kia Strikes. Best on the East Coast."

Click.

"Fiyah, a new producer from Atlanta that I am having flown in to help us cut two singles for our demo. He's new, but my sources say he's dope."

Click.

Marisol gasped as a smiling photo of her filled the screen.

"Marisol aka MariMari, choreographer," Starr said.

Marisol clapped excitedly.

Click.

"Dionne aka Diva DiDi—rapper."

"That's whassup," Dionne said, nodding her head in agreement.

Click.

"Starr aka Starr, of course—lead singer and songwriter."

"Do di-vahhhh," Marisol said with three snaps in the air.

Click.

A small image appeared on-screen and grew in size as a dope beat filled the room through the surround sound. With a boom, an image of a star filled the entire screen, with *Go Gettas* written in graffiti.

More than satisfied with her presentation and the team she'd pulled together in just a few days, Starr walked to the front of the theater. "We are the Go Gettas, ladies, and our team should help us deliver," she said emphatically.

Starr hit the remote. The lights came on, the music faded, and the screen went black just before the pale gold curtains *whooshed* closed.

"Deliver what to who?" Marisol asked, rising to fix herself a frosted Jamaican-Me-Crazy ice.

"A demo to my daddy," she said. "I'm Cole Lester's little girl, but he is all about his business. So we got to come correct to make this happen."

"And you did all this since when?" Dionne asked.

"Three days ago."

"Wow," Dionne and Marisol said in unison.

Wealth and fame definitely had its privileges.

eight

Dionne
October 18@10:43 a.m.| Mood: Cautious

The air was definitely getting cooler and Dionne was glad to have on her new Burberry puffer coat as she walked out of the high-rise building into the fall chill.

"Have a good day, Miss Hunt," Jodfrey, the doorman, said to her, as he held open the rear door of the Town Car waiting for her.

Dionne smiled at him. "Keep it light, J," she said playfully before climbing into the rear of the car.

The older gentleman, who resembled a rosy-cheeked Santa Claus, winked and closed the door securely. She gave him one final wave through the window before the car pulled away from the upscale high-rise apartment building and into the busy Manhattan traffic.

"Good afternoon, Miss Hunt," the driver said.

"Hello."

Dionne recognized the driver but didn't know his name. He wasn't Yuri, the chauffeur who usually shuttled her back and forth from Pace in Saddle River to Newark every day. Her father's assistant, Mindy, would usually take her home to Newark once her weekend visit with her father was over. But her father and his entourage had left that morning for a twelve-city tour overseas. Dionne would have loved to go along, but her mom vetoed *that* idea quickly. School trumped everything as far as Risha Hunt was concerned.

Dionne settled back and flipped through the latest issue of one of the hip-hop magazines. Her dad was on the cover and there was a nice three-page interview with him. She'd found it on the edge of her bed when she got up this morning with a note that said: "Check out ya boy!"

She really was proud of her dad going from hustling a crappy nine-to-five by day and working on his music at night, to being one of the most respected rappers in the game. *Can I live up to that?* she wondered, settling back in the leather seat and crossing the Coach ankle boots she wore.

They'd spent the whole night at Starr's playing the track and working on dance moves, and then she'd spent the day with her dad shopping so she hadn't even had time to try to write a rhyme yet.

Dionne dug the BlackBerry her dad had gotten her yesterday out of her oversize handbag. He'd told her that Sidekicks had been *side-kicked* to the curb. She unlocked the screen and scrolled the tracking ball to the Word to Go app. *If Drake can write rhymes on his BlackBerry, so can I,* she thought.

By the time they'd made the thirty-minute drive to Newark, Dionne's screen was still blank. Sighing, she gathered up her Coach saddlebag as the car pulled to a stop in front of the three-family house where she lived. Feeling very Starr-like, she waited for her driver to open her door before she exited.

"Thanks," she said as he removed her carry-on travel bag and set it down in front of her.

Dionne rushed up the stairs and inside the apartment building. She was anxious to talk to her mom and see if she'd made a decision about the house. "Hey, Ma," she said, closing the front door behind her as she rushed over to hug her mother, who was sitting on the sofa.

"There's my mini-me," Risha said, using the remote to turn the TV volume down.

"Lifetime?" Dionne asked, taking off her coat and sitting down to unzip her boots.

"You know it."

Her mom loved, loved, loved those woe-is-me movies that the cable channel played. Dionne thought they were depressing. They were always, "I'm on the run from my—fill in the blank—abusive husband, alcoholic husband, secret-life-having husband, Mafioso husband."

"Sooo, did you decide on a house?" Dionne asked as nonchalantly as she could.

"Not yet," Risha replied, not bothering to take her eyes off the twenty-inch television. Dionne had offered to trade her forty-inch flat screen, but her mom wasn't hearing it.

Dionne knew not to push. She was already anxious thinking Miss Independent would flip and decide not to pick a house at all. "You cook?" she asked, rising to her feet and grabbing her boots, coat, keys and rolling carry-on bag.

"Barbecue chicken, cabbage and macaroni and cheese," she said as Dionne was walking down the short hallway to her room. "Oh, and Hassan just left. I'm surprised you didn't see him. I think he and his little boo broke up."

Dionne came to an abrupt halt. She slammed into her wall. "Okay," she said casually, like she didn't really care.

Whateva.

She had thought she was over her crush on Hassan, since she didn't want to bring him into her now-fabulous world and have him expose her life as less than fabulous before her father made it big.

As soon as she walked into her room, which could fit inside Starr's closet, Dionne dumped all her stuff on the bed, rummaging through it to find her BlackBerry. "Sugar honey is tasty," she said, stomping her foot at the missed call.

Hassan was #1 on her Hot Boys List and she knew there was no way that the cute football player would stay a free agent for long. And then what? Sit back and think of him kissing another girl the way he'd kissed her? All soft and sweet with just enough pressure to leave a tingling sensation on her lips, but not so much to make Dionne feel like they needed to get a room. Dionne was so out of her lane and headed toward losing her virginity, and Hassan's kiss made her believe he understood that.

Call him back, Dionne! She slid across the floor and closed her door before she hit Hassan back on his cell.

"Whaddup, Di?" he said, his voice slightly raspy.

She held the BlackBerry away from her face as she pursed her lips and breathed in and out. *Calm down, Dionne. Get your ish together.*

"Hey, Has. My moms said you came by looking for me?"

"I feel like some pancakes. Wanna go with me to IHOP?"

Dionne paced in the small area beside her bed. "What about Jalisha?" she asked, her entire body on edge, her heart beating, her pulse racing. She was all nerves, straight crushing.

"We're not together no more."

Good. Perfect. Fab-u-lous.

"Aww… What happened? You know what, never mind. We can talk about it over a stack," she said, already opening her closet to find something extracute to wear.

"I'll be there in about fifteen minutes. Cool?"

"Yeah, uh-huh," Dionne said, distracted as she hung up the phone and tossed her BlackBerry on top of the pile on her bed.

She pulled out a black sheer ruffle shirt, a tailored blazer and dark denims with patent leather flats and a ton of long silver and pearl chains and necklaces. She wanted to be cas', but ever so cute. Ultra-feminine cute. "Ma!" Dionne yelled.

"What?!"

"Come here!" Dionne reached in her closet again and pulled out an off-the-shoulder, striped sweater in bright colors, with a white tank, another pair of dark denims and hot-pink knee-high rainboots. Laid-back cute.

Her moms stuck her head in the door. "What do you want?" she asked, the cordless phone in her hand.

"Who you on the phone with?" Dionne asked, her eyes shifting back to her two outfits.

"Can you give me back my business?"

Dionne looked at her mother. Her brows lowered at the twinkle in her mother's eye and the happy look on her face—that plus the secrecy? "Why do you have that goofy face?" she asked.

"No reason."

Dionne eyed her mother long and hard.

Her mom had had boyfriends before, but mostly it had always been just the two of them. No creepy dude pretending to be nice to show off for her mother, or chilling with his Timbs on their end table, or at their dinner table, or ordering her around, or moving in and making their small but stylish and *clean* apartment smell like feet and farts. Ew.

"Dionne, what did you call me for?" Risha asked, holding the phone to her chest.

"Hassan and I are going to IHOP. Which outfit?" she asked.

"I like the colorful one," she said, turning to head back to the living room.

"Tell whoever it is that your daughter says hello," Dionne called out after her mother.

"What-ev-er," Risha said, mocking Dionne.

Dionne eyed the outfits again. It was IHOP, but she really wanted to do a little extra to let Hassan know she cared what he thought.

Ultra-feminine cute it is, she thought, hurrying to get out of her clothes.

Dionne took the quickest shower ever, mostly to refresh her body since she'd showered at her dad's before she left. She wasted a few precious, but oh so important, moments putting on moisturizer, blush and her favorite shade of Pretty in Pink lip gloss. It definitely was Beauty-on-the-Go 101.

Back in her room, Dionne was just sliding her foot into a pair of Vuitton loafers when their doorbell rang. She emptied the contents of her Coach bag into a black patent leather Hobo bag and flew out the room. "I'll be back," Dionne said to her mother over her shoulder before she pulled the front door closed behind her and then jogged down the stairs of the dimly lit hall.

"Wow. You look really good," Hassan said, nodding his head as he licked his lips and reached out for her hand to twirl her on the porch.

Success! "Thanks," she said shyly, wishing she completely understood the way Hassan made her feel so excited and numb all at once. "You look good, too."

"My swag on ten?" he asked, smiling and smoothing his hands over his face in the long-sleeved dark blue and white plaid shirt he wore with the darkest blue denims and crisp blue and white Jordans that looked straight out of the box.

No hoodie. Thank God! "Most def," she told him, enjoying the feel of his shoulder and arm lightly touching hers as the cab jostled them every time they hit a pothole or bump in the road.

"What happened with Jalisha?" she asked, ever so grateful she sounded straight even though her heart was beating mad crazy.

"She wasn't you."

Dionne's glossy mouth opened with a light gasp as a shiver went across her body.

In that moment she thought of this short-lived group called Fatty Koo who had a show on BET a few years ago. She had loved their slow jam "Chills" but until that exact moment she hadn't even begun to understand it.

You give me chills...up and down my spine.

"Oh, yeah?" Dionne said, not even hiding her grin. "That's what's up."

"Nah, nah, you what's up," he said, bumping his shoulder against hers.

"You flirting hard, Has," she said, turning her head to look into his eyes.

"Thanks for finally noticing," he joked, as the taxi pulled up in front of the International House of Pancakes.

"I haven't been to IHOP in sooo long," she admitted, thinking of how even a casual spot like Cooley's was upscale with its design and menu of celebrity-named dishes.

"You haven't been around a lot of things for sooo long," Hassan said, looking down at her as he held the door open for her.

Dionne looked up at him as she walked past. "Stop complaining. I'm here. You're here."

"Whaddup, Has. You made it."

Dionne's eyes widened at the ten pairs of eyes focused on them as Has stepped forward to slap hands with Nicolas, a short and pudgy dude she remembered from their elementary school.

"You know I was coming through," Has said, white teeth flashing against his chocolate skin.

They're all here, she thought with big-time disappointment, looking at the large group of teenagers lounging in the small waiting area.

Some she recognized. Some she didn't.

Some seemed okay with her presence, waving and smiling. Some didn't, shooting her daggers and glancing sideways—mostly the girls.

Dionne felt big-time overdressed.

It definitely wasn't the cozy, oohsome-twosome she was expecting with just her and Has. The hostess led them to the back where they pushed several tables together to accommodate all twelve of them.

"You a'ight?" Hassan asked, leaning close to her ear.

Chills. Up and down my spine.

She swallowed hard, nodding. "I'm good. I'm just really hungry."

A couple of the girls at the other end of the table giggled. When Dionne looked up they were all looking down the length of the table at her.

"Sound like a dang-on white girl," one of them whispered loud enough for her to hear.

"Miss Oreo," another one said.

"O-kay."

She heard their exaggerated whispers. Dionne's heart pounded. They *were* talking about her.

"Can we say overdressed?"

"Got on my grandmama's going-to-church pearls."

"O-kay."

Hassan was so busy cutting up and cracking jokes with his friends that he didn't even notice how quiet she was. In that moment, the difference in her two worlds seemed larger than ever.

nine

Marisol
October 19@3:45 p.m.| Mood: Happy

"This is our table from now on."

Marisol paused before taking another spoonful of yogurt to look over at Percy, who was getting ready to devour a Diddy dog with a side of Chilli fries. "So we're a couple now?" she asked, crossing her ankles underneath the circular all-white table as she tilted her head and angled her eyes up to look at him—full-on flirt mode, straight from the pages of Seventeen.com.

"Oh, I didn't do it all official. I got you. I got you," he said, smiling hard.

Marisol waited for him to do or say something but minutes later she realized his focus was on his food. "Is it true you live in your parents' guesthouse—by yourself? With a separate entrance?" she asked him in disbelief.

There were plenty of students at Pace living lives most teenagers would only dream about, but turning a teenage boy loose with his own house where anyone could come and go and his parents had *no* clue? That had to be urban legend from the halls of Pace Academy.

Percy nodded like it was nothing.

Marisol's mouth dropped open, but she recovered quickly, filling it with her plastic spoon. Her mother would never go for that, never. Yasmine Rivera believed kids should be closely supervised to help prevent them from turning out like the Heathers of the world.

"Are you and Jordan friends?" she asked suddenly.

"Jordan Jackson?" Percy asked.

Marisol nodded as she reached up to twist her riot of ebony curls into a loose topknot. Her large hoops really swayed from her lobes after freeing them from her hair.

"We're not friends but he's a'ight. We're cool. Why?" Percy asked. "Y'all used to talk?"

Marisol rolled her eyes. "*No.* I just heard something about him. Thought you could confirm or deny."

"Nah, I don't know him like that."

They fell silent and Marisol looked out the window at the few cars passing by.

"You ever wonder what life would be like if your dad wasn't a big-time athlete and all that?" she asked, her eyes locking on a woman completely dressed in white passing by with her dog.

"Boring," he said without question.

Marisol shifted her eyes to him. "But when you have to hear the press trying to knock him for stuff like a bad game or rumors or that dumb ish or the way being a celebrity affects having a normal life, boring doesn't seem so bad to me."

Percy leaned in toward her across the table. "But I

wouldn't have shaken hands with Michael Jordan or talked to Tiger Woods or tossed a ball with Terrell Owens."

It was true that being a celebrity opened a lot of doors and provided access to a lot of different worlds.

"So if you had the chance you wouldn't be famous?" Percy asked, pushing away his now-empty plate.

Marisol shrugged. "I don't know, but I do know that I love my family and nothing comes before that."

Percy's eyes flittered over her face.

Oh my God, booger alert? I will just die!

"A lot of boys in school like you," he said.

Marisol felt her shoulders relax. She still lightly and covertly brushed her finger across her nose just in case. "Not true," she finally answered.

Percy nodded. "Boys are just scared to approach you and your little clique," he said. "They don't want to be the talk of school for getting shot down by one of y'all."

She could see that. They were a little over-the-top in everything they did. From the clothes they wore to the way they completely took over the first-floor girls' bathroom at their whim. "And what about you?"

He leaned back and began to brush his waves with a cocky look in his eye. "I ain't never scared," he said, imitating Lil' Jon.

Marisol leaned back in her chair and nodded.

"O-kaaay," they said in unison, and then burst out laughing, drawing the curious stares of other diners.

"I better get to practice," he said, rising from his seat to pull his book bag onto his broad shoulders before he motioned for their waitress. "If we're late, coach makes us run laps."

She took her aviator shades from the hard protective case and slid them on before she rose to tie her scarf around her neck and slide on her Ralph Lauren peacock coat.

She didn't miss his eyes on her as he stuck a toothpick in his mouth.

Marisol played like she didn't see or feel his eyes on her. If there was one thing Marisol knew she had a lock on, it was knowing what looks, colors and style fit her best. She looked good and he knew it.

Percy paid their bill with a credit card and they left Cooley's together, walking side by side once they were out the door.

"You're coming to see me play Friday?" he asked, shifting to walk on the other side of her nearest the street.

A gentleman. Her mother would like that.

Marisol shifted her cinnamon eyes to him. Friday she had Go Gettas practice.

Hmm. Practice with my friends? Go and support my boo? Well, almost boo? Future boo? Whatevs.

Practice or the game?

Practice or the game?

"So I would be the Melanie to your Derwin?" Marisol asked, stalling as her head and her heart continued to debate.

Percy frowned. "Who?"

"From the TV show *The Game.* Derwin the football player and Melanie his fiancée?" she said, like "duh."

Percy looked shocked. "You wanna get married?" he

asked, his eyes as big as two small cups of Pinkberries frozen yogurt.

Marisol eyed him curiously. "Umm, no, I do not want to get married. I was just saying… You know what, never mind."

Percy just shrugged.

Marisol turned her attention back to her ongoing tug of war. Practice? Game?

Honestly, she was excited about being the choreographer for the group and even more pleased that Starr had faith in her and did not hire some choreographer to the stars to get the job done. She had already been working hard to come up with some of the moves she could teach them.

On the other hand…

Marisol looked up at Percy with the fall winds swirling around them as they crossed the street to the dog park. She really wanted to see him play and cheer him on and even have him throw her a kiss or a wink after he scored a touchdown or two.

But she loved dancing and if Starr was able to get this thing rolling for real?

"I might have something to do this Friday," Marisol told him, reaching down to lightly brush her hand across his. "But I will be there next week. Promise. Cool?"

Percy looked disappointed but nodded. "Cool," he said, turning his hand to capture hers tightly.

Marisol liked how it felt. She liked it a lot.

Between texting with Starr, Dionne and Percy, and responding to Facebook friends, Marisol barely got her homework finished before dinner. It was a Rivera tradition that they ate dinner together every night at seven o'clock. No excuses.

Marisol took her seat at the long table across from her brother. She playfully stuck out her tongue at him. He proceeded to rise from his chair and fart. Marisol gagged and covered her nose as he laughed hysterically.

The two of them settled down as their mother strolled into the massive and elegantly decorated dining room looking beautiful in an all-white caftan. "There're my babies," she said in Spanish, as the chef began bringing in steaming dishes of food.

"Where's Daddy?" Marisol asked, her stomach growling at the smell of the Spanish cuisine.

"He had a business meeting," Yasmine said.

As a heaping bowl of stew heavy with chicken, pork and sausage was ladled into her bowl, Marisol's eyes shifted to her mother. After catching her father cheating, she wondered how her mother ever trusted him. How could she not wonder if he was where he said he was?

Sigh.

"The photographers from *Latina* magazine will be here next week to take pictures of the family and the house," Yasmine said in Spanish, stirring her stew but never lifting the spoon to her mouth. "I want you all to make sure your rooms are spotless...especially you, Carlos."

Marisol nodded. "And please open the windows and air out the fart fumes," she drawled sarcastically.

"Marisol, that's not appropriate for the dinner table."

"*Sí,* Mami."

When Marisol saw her brother wiggle his brows at her, she knew another missile had been launched. She decided to ignore him and hopefully the smell. "Mami, I got an A on my dance solo," she said.

Yasmine clapped proudly. "Congratulations. You are a natural dancer…from the Santos side of your family, of course," she said.

"I beg to differ."

They all looked to the door as her father strolled in looking ever so handsome in all black. Marisol's smile couldn't have been any wider as he kissed Yasmine softly on the corner of her mouth, removed Carlos's baseball cap and then tugged Marisol's curls as he moved to take his seat.

She glanced at her mother and could see that she was happy about her father's sudden appearance as well.

Yasmine rose and walked to the middle of the big table to fix her father the largest helping of the stew before placing it in front of him where he sat at the opposite end of the table. He rested his hand on her hip in a casual gesture that reminded Marisol of the innocent way Percy held her hand earlier today.

"Now, the dancing blood is from the Rivera side," her father, Alex, said, his skin even more brown from the natural tan he acquired during baseball season.

"My bruised toes are evidence of your dancing ability, Alejandro," Yasmine said teasingly, moving back to the other end of the table to take her seat.

"That sounds like a challenge. After dinner, you and I will have a dance-off."

Marisol was ecstatic to see them finally getting back to

joking and teasing one another. She was happy because it meant that her father was coming out of his "We're out of the play-offs" funk, and her parents might just be able to enjoy being together again and not just coexisting.

Like Oprah says, there is a difference.

"I can dance, too!" Carlos said as he chewed a mouthful of meat.

That's why he couldn't make it at Pace, Marisol thought, thanking God that her brother attended a different private school for boys after Headmaster Payne expelled him for dying the pond and his hair royal-blue in celebration of their father's team's World Series win two years ago.

Pace had been free of the *pequeño terror* (the little terror) ever since.

"I want in, too, Papi," Marisol said in Spanish, which she rarely used unless at home.

"And for the winner?" Yasmine asked.

"Winner's choice," her father said, his eyes locked on his wife.

"Okay. Ew!" Marisol said with a facial expression that made her parents laugh.

Truthfully, Marisol couldn't be any happier.

ten

Starr

October 20@8:47 a.m.| Mood: Jealous

"We have to win this."

Starr's eyes were locked on the huge and colorful glossy poster positioned below the announcement board in the hallway of Pace. Dionne and Marisol looked over her shoulder to look at the poster for themselves.

"A talent show?" Marisol asked, taking in the huge microphone in the center of the graphic of a shining star. "In two weeks?"

Starr shifted her eyes from Marisol to Dionne.

"You're trippin'. We're not ready for that," Marisol protested.

Starr sighed. "Do I always have to be the ear, the shoulder and the spine for the three of us?" she snapped, her eyes flashing. "We have nothing to fear but fear itself."

"Look who's been paying attention in history class," Marisol mumbled under her breath.

Other students began to gather around the Pacesetters and the announcement board. Starr grabbed her friends' hands.

"Excuse us," she said loudly over the excited murmur of the students.

The crowd parted like the Red Sea.

The girls walked right on through. Starr turned the corner and headed straight down the hall to the first-floor ladies' bathroom. Her Manolos faltered as she took in Jordan and Heather sitting together on the windowsill at the end of the hall.

Enough morning light came through the glass and highlighted the couple as Jordan squeezed Heather's hand. "How touching," Starr snapped, her eyes taking in Heather's fullness—breasts, hips and thighs, in her denim jumpsuit.

Heather made Starr's body look like a boy's with all its video-vixen-like dips and curves. Obviously that was what Jordan wanted.

Starr couldn't stand the sight of either one of them. It was funny how thin the line was between crush and disgust. She hitched her head higher, knowing her girls were looking at her for her reaction. Starr was planning on delivering a performance worthy of an Oscar.

If he'd rather have the worn-down cow over the tender cut of filet mignon then eat away because Starr wasn't serving up *her* goodies anyway. If Heather wanted to keep her legs open more than a twenty-four-hour Walgreens then she could have a ball. But Starr didn't play follow the leader.

"Hey, Starr—"

Starr paused and shot Heather a fierce look that made the poor desperate-to-fit-in child immediately clamp her mouth shut. The look she gave Jordan was filled with the animosity she had for him. For the past two weeks he'd tried to talk to her, but as far as she was concerned her life was Facebook and he was BLOCKED.

Marisol and Dionne continued into the bathroom and Starr reached in her satchel for their fake Out of Order sign, slapping it on the door as she continued to shoot them both hate lasers.

"Starr—"

But she held up her hand, stopping Jordan before he could even begin, and then walked into the bathroom.

"Oh my God, do you think they were talking about child support and Pampers?" Marisol asked, stepping in front of the triptych of floor-length mirrors in the corner.

Dionne plopped down onto one of the two chaise longues, her eyes on the wall mural depicting some garden. The light from the crystal chandeliers reflected against her upturned face. "That's the craziest mess I ever heard, Marisol."

Starr shook her head. "I cannot believe Jordan is throwing his life away like this," she said, hurt beyond words. Seeing him around school just brought it all back—the hope of a crush, and the disappointment when it goes nowhere.

She hated that she so clearly remembered the day he sang to her in the athletic building—*that* Jordan, she thought would be hers. This one with a baby on the way—she didn't know him at all.

"Especially with a record contract with your dad. That's major and I hope he can stay on track," Dionne said.

The bathroom door opened and they all turned ready to blow away whoever had been bold enough to come in once they had posted their Out of Order sign. They were surprised when Jordan walked in.

"You can't come in here," Starr said, whispering as if the headmaster had a listening device hidden in the bathroom.

"And you can't hold a bathroom hostage every time the three of you want to gossip," he said, his voice angry.

"I can do whatever the hello and goodbye I want to do, Jordan Jackson…including ignoring you," Starr said, crossing the room to step in his face.

"Ignore me for what, Starr?" he asked, not backing down from her. "You didn't use to ignore me. Huh? What? Did you? Huh? No?"

Starr's hands went into fists at her sides and she gave him a straight-on Aunt Esther one-eyed stare. "That's when I was too dumb to know you were around here picking up sex cooties and making babies with the local 'welcome to my vagina squad' at Pace."

"Oooh," Marisol and Dionne said in unison, making ugly faces.

Jordan threw his hands up in the air. "I did not sleep with Heather and I don't have a baby on the way," he screamed.

Starr's hair flew back from the air he released. "Liar!" she roared back.

"O-M-G," Marisol said.

Dionne's mouth was wide-open.

The bathroom door opened again and Heather flew in.

"Hellooo. I'm not pregnant!" she said, holding up a used pregnancy test.

Flat line.

Starr would have gladly crossed her arms over her chest

and went peacefully to her Maker for the foolishness she was in the midst of.

Jordan covered his head with his hands.

"No, she didn't," Dionne said to Marisol, talking out of the side of her mouth.

Marisol nodded and curled her lips. "Yes, mami. Yes, she did."

"First off. Ew! Ew! Ew!" Starr held her hand up to Heather. "Don't come near me with *that*."

Dionne stepped forward, her cotton-candy-painted nails held high. "Listen, it said in *Teen Vogue*—"

"Oh Lord," Jordan sighed, turning around to hit his fist on the wall.

Dionne looked aghast at his response. "What you got against *Teen Vogue?*" she snapped in a high-pitched voice.

Jordan just dropped his head against the wall.

"Um, Heather, you can put down your pee-ridden pregnancy stick now," Marisol added calmly. "I can confirm the negative sign. Okay? *Gracias*."

Heather dropped her arm.

Starr felt like she was starring in a sitcom. She was looking for Ice Cube or Tyler Perry to jump out of one of the stalls and hand her a check. "We're out of here," she said, snatching her Louis Vuitton messenger bag before she strolled into the hallway, taking long strides like she was headed to war. Dionne and Marisol were right behind her, with Marisol clutching their Out of Order sign.

Their heels hit the tiled floors in perfect unison as they made their way down the hall like Charlie's Angels.

Starr said nothing—absolutely nothing—as she processed everything that had happened.

They reached their lockers.

"At least Heather's not pregnant," Dionne said. "You ever see that show on MTV, *16 and Pregnant?* Like, seriously, who wants to go through that?"

Starr busied herself freshening up her makeup and composing herself.

"I would've just taken her word for it without flinging pee all around from her little stick," Marisol joked.

That eased Starr's mood and she broke down and laughed with her friends.

"Starr. Pssst. Starr. Staarrrr."

From her seat in between her mother and father, Starr tried hard to ignore Malcolm or Martin from the rear seat behind her.

"Starrrr!"

The entire family was headed to a dinner party at someone's house. They were in the bulletproof Denali with two of her father's burly security guards in the front seat. She was in the middle row with her parents and the twins were in the rear seat.

Her father was taking calls from all three of his cell phones.

Her mother was listening to a track a producer wanted her to use on her new album.

Starr was being big-time aggravated by her brothers taking turns calling her name like a thirsty man begging for water.

"Staaaaaaaarrrrr."

"Answer your brothers," Cole Lester said, covering his iPhone with his hand.

Starr froze. "Daddy?" she said in disbelief.

They were being annoying and *she* got riffed on? *Life is such a dollar store sometimes.*

Starr turned around in her seat and the twins both began to giggle, holding their chubby hands over their mouths, wearing matching outfits.

"What?" she snapped.

Malcolm's or Martin's eyes widened. "Starr mad at choo," he said, pointing at his mirror image.

"Not me. Choo," Martin or Malcolm said, pointing back at his twin.

They both turned to look at her with the biggest eyes ever. "We're sorry. We love you, Starr," they said in unison, their chubby fingers reaching out to her.

She rolled her eyes. She couldn't stay mad at the little crumb-snatchers. Turning around a bit more on her seat, she reached back and squeezed their hands.

They smiled broadly.

Starr could only shake her head as she turned back around to face the front windshield while smoothing the large above-the-knee-length skirt of her asymmetrical, one-shoulder dress. Her cropped leather jacket and Gucci ankle boots gave the dress a youthful, slightly edgy feel.

"You have reached your destination."

Starr looked up at the sound of the OnStar GPS. Their Denali pulled up to a huge wrought-iron gated entrance that led to a slightly sloped, brick-paved driveway that fronted a beautifully lit house on the top of a hill. *Wow!* It took a lot to impress Starr Lester, and this place took her breath away.

Once the gates opened and they cruised up the driveway she saw more and more of the palatial estate that included a helicopter sitting on the concrete pad in the distance. The mansion was the same size of theirs if not bigger.

She couldn't wait to get inside.

As soon as they pulled up in front of the massive brick structure a tuxedo-clad valet opened the passenger door. Starr climbed out with the help of the bodyguards and stood at the bottom step of the veranda.

She liked that her father stepped out of the car to help her mother out. Kinda like, "This is my woman. I *got* this." Plus, the way her mom was looking, Starr couldn't blame him for wanting to be so attentive.

Sasha, an R&B icon, was a triple threat: her voice, her looks and her body. In the body-hugging Givenchy dress she wore, the first talent didn't even matter. She had curves for days. The knee-length hem of the dress emphasized her legs, while the ruffles down the center of the dress emphasized her curves all the more.

Their stylist, FiFi, had done very well. Tasteful jewelry, just the right makeup and her hair in an updo.

My mom is the ish, Starr thought as she watched her mother as she turned to take each of her brothers' chubby hands in hers.

They walked up the stairs, their bodyguard falling back a respectful distance as the double doors opened. Starr half expected to hear an angelic "aaaaaah."

She looked past the shoulders of the tuxedo-clad balding white man and his red-haired wife who towered over him by at least a foot—maybe a foot and a half. "Welcome partner," the man said, shaking Cole's hand vigorously. "How does it feel to be the owner of a football team?"

"Feels damn good," Cole said as her mother and the man's wife quickly exchanged air kisses.

Starr stiffened as she caught a glimpse of the hem of a pale gold sequined dress coming down the massive staircase leading to the upper levels. As they all moved inside the foyer, Starr kept her eyes trained on the dress. She soon recognized it as Gucci...of course. No one knew Gucci better than her—no one.

Starr's face tightened and then nearly cracked as Natalee Livingston's face appeared. *This is her house,* Starr thought, through her fake smile as she eyed the tall white teenaged girl with a riot of bright red curls. Game recognizes game, style recognizes style and Starr knew this girl was her equal.

"Hi, Starr," she said, her husky voice seeming incongruous with a teenage girl, just as it did the first time Starr met her.

"Starr, you know Natalee," Mrs. Livingston said. "You two should catch up."

Starr felt a hand lightly massage the stiffness from her thin shoulder. She caught the subtle hint of her mother's perfume. "Yes, especially since Natalee might be attending Pace Academy soon," Sasha said.

Competition for me at my school? Nooooo! she mentally screamed.

Pace Academy

The Way I See It!

HUSTLENOMICS/BABYWATCH

Posted in *uncategorized* on October 20@12:02 a.m. by thedivaofdish

Hmm. Someone still fresh to the halls of Pace Academy has a part-time job braiding hair. I guess you thought I would say something droll like, is her rapper daddy on the repo list for his extravagant cars and jewelry. Nope. Actually I'm proud of her. Maybe she has more to her than clothes, lip gloss and the smell of Starr Lester's butt on her nose.

Okay, baby watch is over. Pace Academy maintains its 0% graduation rate for teen mothers (side-eye on the total lack of reality on that). Anyway SHE isn't preggers and has been carrying around a negative pregnancy test all day to prove it. One word, honey: TRASH. (I'll leave it up to you to decide if I'm talking about her or the used pregnancy stick.)

Smooches,
Pace Academy's Diva of Dish

50 comments

eleven

Dionne
October 21@5:47 a.m.| Mood: Scared

Dionne was still trying to pinch herself to make sure she wasn't dreaming. Her eyes went from her mother's mouth moving a mile a minute to her father throwing in his dime whenever he got a chance. They both were teaming up to get on her. *Now they want to get along,* she thought, leaning back into the sofa of her father's living room as they stood over her.

Her mom was still in her hospital uniform, her two pairs of earrings clanging together overtime as she worked her head.

Her dad was in his usual attire of denims and a black wife beater. Diamond chains swinging, denims hanging low, diamond grill in place, shades in place even though there wasn't a bit of sunlight in sight.

All of this because she'd asked for permission to spend the night at Starr's tomorrow even though it wasn't her week to be with her dad. Her mother casually asked why. Dionne casually answered that they were practicing for their new singing group.

And, boy, did the ish hit the fan right then.

One phone call to her dad and a wide-open ride to New York in their Honda and, *ta-da,* she was in the middle of a parent sandwich, catching hell from both sides.

"What happened to you wanting to be a lawyer, Dionne? Huh? What happened?" Risha asked. "Huh? Huh? Huh?"

"Ma, pleeeaaase. Oh my god," Dionne yelled, her frustration spilling over.

Dionne clamped her hand over her mouth. *Uh-oh.*

Risha's arched eyebrow shot up. "Who do you think you talking to, Dionne?" she asked, completely fired up.

Lahron stepped in between them. "A'ight, ladies. Chill. Just breathe and relax," he said, his voice raspy.

"I'm sorry, Ma," Dionne began. "But you're acting like me being in music group is going to change my plans. I can still go to college."

Risha threw up her hands. "Lawd, take me now," she wailed dramatically.

"Rish, yo, let me holler at my daughter for a sec," he said, hitching his pants up before sitting down next to Dionne.

Her eyes went in between the two, raising her finger to point at both. "You're right, *your* daughter. *My* little girl wanted to be a lawyer. Fix this, *Lahron the Don,*" she said sarcastically before she reached down and flicked his Gucci shades from his face.

"Ain't a bit of sun," she muttered before she walked out of the living room and into the kitchen, still fussing.

Dionne reached down and picked the shades up to hand to her dad. He took them and laughed as he set them on the leather end table. "Your mama stays on ten. She always ready to blast."

Dionne smiled. "Always."

"You almost got your head chopped off right then," he said.

"I'm sorry. I didn't mean to be disrespectful."

"Huh. Group my behind. She better group them grades and get her butt in college if she know like I know. 'Round here, losing her mind, yelling at me. I can bring her back to reality. I can bring her back real quick. Trust and believe that," Risha said, still fussing aloud in the kitchen.

Dionne and her dad exchanged a look.

"I'm not the one you need to apologize to," her father said.

Dionne nodded, reaching up to massage her scalp with her fingertips. "I will."

"Now tell me about this group you in."

Dionne sat up. "It's me, Starr and Marisol," she said.

Lahron scratched his chin giving his daughter a side-eye. "Tell me something I don't know."

"True," she agreed. Who else would she be in a group with but her girls?

Dionne explained their plans, their roles in the group and the dream team Starr put together. "But we don't have a record deal or nothing. Even Starr said her dad didn't play when it came to his business and if we weren't on point, he wouldn't even mess with it."

"This industry is way more than you kids get to see firsthand," Lahron said, moving his diamond-encrusted microphone up and down the chain. "To be honest I don't want that for you. I don't want you to get caught up in that mess. Your moms and I had plans for you. Even when we have beef with each other we never lose focus of wanting the best for you. I don't know if this is it."

Dionne was surprised by his words and his serious tone. Her father was always the easygoing one and the one to give her the world even if it cost him his last dime.

"It's just for fun right now," she said softly, trying to convince him. "And you know Mr. Lester's not going to let anything crazy happen to us."

Lahron pressed his elbows into his knees and folded his hands in the air between them. He said nothing.

Dionne knew he was going back and forth with it. "I promise my grades won't drop and I will go to college regardless of what happens."

Lahron looked over at his daughter. "Let me sleep on it and talk to your moms some more. I'm not saying yes—" he continued.

"But you didn't say no, Daddy," she said, allowing herself to get excited as she jumped over and hugged his neck.

"The important question is, can you spit?" he asked, leaning back to look up at her.

Bashfully, Dionne looked at the ceiling and shrugged.

Lahron closed his eyes and shook his head with a groan.

The next day Dionne sat down on the metal stairs leading up to the second floor of the sports complex. She hit Send on the last text to all her hair-braiding clients notifying them that she was out of business. It was just too risky.

At the beginning of the school year the headmaster had called her into his office to give her a letter for her parents. One good snoop and she'd discovered her father hadn't paid her thirty-thousand-dollar tuition. Embarrassing.

Thinking he'd been about to fall into the growing category of rappers-who-get-rich-quick-and-spend-it-even-quicker, she had cut back on her shopping and even started braiding hair for pocket money. It had been her way of helping her daddy for all he did for her before and after his rise to fame.

But Dionne had told her clients to keep their lips zipped and obviously somebody couldn't hold water—i.e. they talked too much.

Before her dad hit platinum with his music, Dionne had always wanted to work and make her own money, even though her mom wanted her to focus on school.

She hadn't really thought about it until that nicely worded letter, with its veiled threat of her expulsion, was sent home. That had caused one helluva argument between her parents.

"There goes my baby..."

Dionne was just headed to her art appreciation class when her ringtone sounded. She looked down at the picture of her and Hassan hugged up outside IHOP together.

"Hey, you," she said, reaching down to swipe dust from her favorite cherry-red Vuitton loafers.

"What you doing?"

Trying not to die of embarrassment. "About to head to lunch."

"Yeah, me, too."

Silence.

"Something wrong, Dionne?" he asked.

She shook her head like he could see her. "Nope."

"Let's go to the movies tonight."

Dionne perked up, but her spirits were shot back down. "I can't. I have practice tonight," she said.

After begging and pleading with her parents to let her stay in the group, they'd given in. But there were big-time stipulations like keeping up her grades, staying on track for college, no profanity, sexy music or nasty dancing.

"Practice for what?"

"Me and a couple of my friends are starting a group," she admitted.

"So my baby gonna be famous?" he asked, sounding excited for her.

"We're just getting started so I don't know 'bout all that."

Famous? Like the next Destiny's Child? Her mind hadn't even gone that far yet. She was just working up the nerve to be able to write sixteen bars to fit the song Starr was supposed to write.

"Don't forget about me when you give your acceptance speech at the BET Awards," he joked.

Whoa! BET Awards. Acceptance speech. His brain was moving faster than Starr's.

"I had to beg my parents to let me be in the group," Dionne admitted, looking up as the doors to the building opened and a group of teenagers walked in and then noisily jogged up the stairs.

"Your dad, too?"

"Yup."

"Crucial."

Dionne smiled. She'd forgotten how *crucial* was slang for everything back in eighth grade.

"I'll be home tomorrow night and we can catch a flick then," she said, not caring that she sounded hopeful. She made the choice to go for Hassan. Somehow she would find a way to make it work.

"Okay. That's whassup," he said. "Lunch is almost over. I'll call you later."

"Okay."

She ended the call, thinking of him looking good and catching the eyes of plenty of girls at school. For the first time she kinda regretted going to a different school than Hassan. And after the Diva of Dumb called her out with that hair-braiding ish, Dionne was trying to remember why she was at Pace, too.

She grabbed her pocketbook and jogged down the steps to walk out the door and into the cold air. She pulled her jacket collar around her ears to shield her from the swirling winds and made her way to the main hall.

"Hey, Dionne! Wait up."

She turned and looked as Eric caught up to her. They had talked briefly around the time Starr was planning her big birthday bash. He was someone who fit in with her life at Pace, but she never forgot about Hassan. Plus Eric's text had started to creep her out, making her think that he was a major perv.

They'd actually made up at Starr's party and he'd promised to not be such a horny toad. That lasted all of two days before he'd called her one night and wanted to know what she was wearing—if anything. Ugh!

She gave him a brief wave and turned to keep it moving to the cafeteria. No time for his mess, she thought, as she breezed through the doors of the caf.

Dionne paused as all eyes turned her way. She felt everyone staring at her as she made her way to the table, mindful of keeping her head held high. "What did y'all get for lunch?" she asked, as if she didn't have a care in the world.

Starr pushed her asymmetrical bang away from her eyes. "A blogful of gossip," she answered, slightly caustic.

"I wonder who she is talking about," Dionne said, removing her denim trench before she grabbed a handful of grapes from Marisol's tray.

Marisol and Starr exchanged a brief look.

"It's not you?" Marisol asked.

Dionne shook her head. "So everything the Diva of Dumb says is gospel now. Y'all really think she's keeping it hundred percent?"

Dionne felt herself relax as the conversation changed to their practice that night and the upcoming talent show.

twelve

Marisol

October 21@7:47 p.m.| Mood: Pissed!

Marisol grabbed a hand towel to wipe the sweat from her neck and face. She had to fight the urge to toss the towel in on the whole Go Gettas plan. She rolled her eyes as she grabbed her water bottle and took a healthy swig as she paced around the polished hardwood floors of the dance studio.

Dionne slumped down on the floor and spread her limbs like she was prepared to make snow angels. "Marisol, girl, I thought I knew how to dance," she gasped. "I can't keep up."

Starr paced in her bright pink shorts and white tank. "I think we can do better on the dance moves," she said, using the remote to turn down the volume on their track.

"Huh?" Dionne asked, surprised by the comment as she lifted her head up from the floor to eye Starr as if she was crazy.

Marisol did a quick ten count as she adjusted the shorts she wore over her leotards. "If you are already struggling to handle the simple dance moves I came up with, why would I make them harder?" she asked, talking slowly.

Starr shook her head. "We're not struggling to learn. I think you're struggling to teach us properly."

Marisol wrung the towel between her hands, pretending it was Starr's neck.

Dionne hopped up. "Maybe we should just focus on getting the song together first. Do you have the lyrics, Starr?"

"Of course," she said, bending over to remove a fuchsia folder.

Marisol fought the urge to put her Nike into Starr's behind. Starr had been just too picky and difficult through Marisol's whole routine as she first ran through the steps alone. It seemed like she complained about every step the whole time.

Who? What? When? Where? And why?

It only got worse when she tried to teach them the steps and they couldn't pick it up. An hour and a half later, and still nothing. And the routine wasn't complicated at all.

I missed Percy's game to hear Starr whine?

"I know it seems like I'm being hard on us. But as soon as anyone catches a whiff that we're doing this, all eyes will be on us—watching, critiquing. We have to have a thick skin, the kind that water rolls right off," Starr said, eyeing them both with determination before she handed them each a piece of paper.

"Marisol, I'm sorry. But please just come up with something that gives us strong stage presence. Let's really work it. 'Kay?"

Like you're working my nerves? Marisol cut her eyes at Dionne. Ever the peacemaker, Dionne just shrugged and focused her attention on the lyrics on the paper.

Marisol had worked hard to choreograph that routine, and for somebody who hadn't even learned it to criticize was big-time annoying. She felt like packing up her stuff, calling her driver and hightailing it to Percy's game.

"Okay, so, I thought the song should be all about us and the things we love—boys and fashion," Starr said, sitting down on one of the leather-upholstered benches along the wall. "Like our theme song. Read it over and tell me what you think."

Go Gettas

Pull up to the party, dressed in my best
All boyz eyes on me, can't settle for less
Took my spot in the middle
Work my hips like a riddle
Your boyz eyes on me, watching me jiggle

Go Gettas…Go Gettas…Yeah.
All the boyz wanna get with me
Go Gettas…Go Gettas…Yeah!
All the girlz wanna chill with me
Go Gettas…Go Gettas…Yeah!

Marisol lifted up the paper. *"Work my hips like a riddle"? What the hello and goodbye does that mean? And why all the* me-me-me? *Where's the* us *and* we *and* our?

She didn't even bother with the next two verses.

"So what do you think?" Starr asked.

Dionne nodded. "I like it, but let's hear it as a song," she suggested.

"Good idea," Starr said, rising to grab the remote and fill the air with the track.

The bass line filled the air and Starr began to bounce her shoulders. "Pull up to the party, dressed in my best. All boyz eyes on me, can't settle for less," Starr sang, closing her eyes as she pointed with her finger.

Marisol frowned. The music was too loud. She could hardly hear her. She looked at Dionne, mouthing, "I can't hear her."

Dionne nodded in agreement.

"Work my hips like a riddle."

Marisol stepped up and picked up the remote from the bench, turning the surround system down.

"Your boyz eyes on me, watching me jiggle."

O-M-G! Marisol mouth dropped wide-open right along with her eyes.

"Go Gettas...Go Gettas...Yeah. All the boyz wanna get with me."

Madre dios, she can't sing. Oh. My. God.

Starr couldn't sing and was obviously tone deaf as she hit a riff that made Marisol cringe and cover her face with the lyrics sheet.

What in the hello and goodbye? Marisol thought.

As the song went on, Starr's singing got worse—the highs, the lows, the missed notes. It was like the first week of *American Idol* when the truly awful singers got most of the airtime.

Marisol eyed Dionne, whose face was just as shocked as hers. "She can't sing," Marisol mouthed.

"Not at all," Dionne mouthed back.

When Starr started dancing to the track, Marisol had to bite her bottom lip to keep from bursting out laughing at Starr from sheer embarrassment for her friend.

As soon as Marisol climbed into the back of her chauffeur-driven car the next day, she called Dionne's phone. The two friends hadn't been able to talk since last night, and neither had the heart to text each other about the performance in front of Starr.

"I was waiting for your call."

Marisol held up her hand, like she was trying to stop traffic. "Okay, what are we going to do?"

Dionne sighed. "We have to tell her. Right?"

"I don't know," she admitted, crossing her legs that were clad in a pair of skinny jeans. "The only thing I do know is that if Starr had to sing to save her life we might as well buy black dresses, *mami*."

Marisol didn't miss the chuckle from her driver.

"You didn't know she couldn't sing?" Dionne asked.

Both of Marisol's eyebrows went up. "I never heard her sing, but her mother is Sasha! Come on, she should have picked some of that up."

"Nope, she missed it all. She didn't get one bit of singing DNA from her mama. Not one bit."

Marisol shifted her eyes to look out the windows as the

car left Bernardsville, New Jersey, to her parents' estate in Upper Saddle River. Suddenly she remembered the talent show. She gasped so deeply that she sounded like a vacuum cleaner just turned on.

The chauffeur eased down on the brakes and turned around. "Are you okay, Miss Rivera?"

"Marisol? You okay?" Dionne asked.

"I'm fine," she told them both.

The chauffeur settled back forward and off the car went.

"Dionne, the talent show? What are we going to do?" she asked.

"I don't want to hurt her feelings."

"Yeah, but we don't want to be the laughingstock of Pace *and* the Diva of Dumb," Marisol insisted.

"Listen, Marisol, I gotta take this call, but I'm going to call you back as soon as I get off the phone," said Dionne of the other line.

"Okay." Marisol locked and then slid her phone into the side pocket of her Birkin tote.

Starr wanted fame so badly that she was ignoring the issue of whether she had talent or not? *Would Mr. Lester actually give them a record deal with Starr howling to the moon like that?* Marisol thought.

Fame wasn't Marisol's main goal. She loved to dance. Period. In truth her dreams involved standing center stage, in the spotlight, ready to give the performance of her life—the kind of physical and emotional dance that would bring people to their feet. And she didn't care if it was a crowd of two or two million as long as they understood the passion she had for dance.

Fame wasn't her goal in life, especially when she saw how quickly fame became infamy.

"There goes my baby…"

Marisol yawned from their late night of hearing Starr completely kill the music as she pulled her cell back out.

"Hey, you."

Marisol's heart smiled. "Congratulations on your win," she said sweetly, completely crushing.

"I scored two touchdowns. My dad kept the ball," he said, sounding very proud of himself.

"I get the next touchdown football for my desk," she insisted.

"You got it."

They fell silent on the phone and neither rushed to find words. Sometimes at night they fell asleep that way.

"How was your practice?" he asked, filling the silence.

Marisol caught a flashback of Starr hitting a sour note and visibly winced. It seemed to echo in her head. "Long story, short on patience. Let's move on," she said.

"Huh?" he asked, sounding confused. "Move on where?"

Marisol just shook her head. She read in one of her favorite magazines that there was no such thing as the perfect man (or in her case, boy). Percy was *really* cute—like really, really cute—popular, nice build, from a wealthy family, good in sports and on track to follow his father's football legacy.

But bless his heart, Marisol had found his one flaw. He wasn't exactly the sharpest pencil in the box.

thirteen

Starr
October 22@10:47 p.m.| Mood: Inspired

Starr hummed the melody in her head again and again as she twisted her fuzzy-topped pencil in her hand. Now that she had gotten the first song out of the way, she was putting the finishing touches on a ballad—a teenage love song. Everybody loves a good slow jam.

With her vocals and Fiyah's producing talent, the Go Gettas were going to take off. By the time Fiyah arrived from Atlanta next week, she wanted the lyrics done.

She thought about both Marisol and Dionne texting all night. Definitely signs of being boo'ed up. She scribbled on her notepad:

Marisol & Percy
Dionne & Eric
Starr & Nobody :(

Maybe she should write a sad love song. She thought about her argument with Jordan and the rumors about him and Heather. Still her heart just wouldn't let him go.

She drew a big heart in the center of the page and wrote his name in it with a sigh. She shouldn't care that Jordan took the time to confront her about blocking him out of her life right in front of Heather, The Hoochie. She shouldn't feel totally breathless whenever she passed him in the hallway at school. She shouldn't. But she did—totally.

She pushed her bangs away from her face, easing her hair behind her ear as she tapped the notebook with her pencil and hummed the slow track Fiyah had emailed her.

Starr wrote down lyrics like the pencil was directly connected to her heart. She erased them. She scratched out lines until there were holes in the page.

My heart…just won't let go
My feelings for you…they must grow
My love…it's hard not to show
Because my heart won't go
My heart…oh no it won't let go
I can't have you, why won't I let go?

Starr stood up from her stool and left the vocal booth to enter the control room. She reached for the button to fill the studio with the achingly sweet track.

"Every day a star is born…every day a star is born."

As her Jay-Z ringtone sounded, Starr went back into the booth to pick up her iPhone from the stool: an email from Indria. As soon as Starr had signed them up for the talent show, she'd immediately asked Indria to find the Go Gettas a performance outfit and a preview outfit. Starr couldn't wait to see what Indria had in mind, moving from the stool to pick up her laptop so that she could view the photos better.

"Every day a star is born," she sang softly as she waited for the photos to download.

Indria had twelve outfits laid out on an all-white background. Starr immediately saw that there was lots of color and she was happy. Her eyes skimmed over everything in the photos.

The performance outfits were vivid, whimsical and fun. The arrival outfits were sleek and stylish with youthful touches. The shoes were all the *bizness.* Just what Starr had wanted!

She texted Indria:

Loving it all. U r the bestest Indria!! :)

And then she forwarded the email to Marisol and Dionne. "Watch them Go Gettas go and get that first prize!!!" she typed, before hitting Send.

Everything about her plan was falling into place.

Well, almost everything, she muttered, picking up her cell phone. Everything on her list of to-dos was on point. Now she needed to get the girls' ish together ASAP.

She texted Dionne first.

Where r u?

Bzzzz.

@ the movies.

Starr frowned deeply, her fingers flying across the keyboard.

Did u work on getting that rap 2gthr?

Bzzzz.

Not yet. I'll hit u up later. Deuces.

Starr didn't bother to respond. Dionne had just ticked her off, chilling at the movies when she should have been getting with her dad and writing sixteen bars. "Am I the only one who wants to do things right?"

She texted Marisol:

R u working on nu routine???!!!!

Bzzzz.

Hanging w/fam.

Starr rolled her eyes, and had to fight the urge not to throw her iPhone across the room. Instead she texted them both:

U 2 need to get like Drake and want to be $ucce$$ful. Ugh. I need a routine that is more J Lo than J Slo and a rap that is tighter than ur weave Dionne. Sigh. My ish is on point. Get on my level.

She paced the floor. Starr wanted this bad. She was born to be a star. She was made for celebrity. She was made to be just as famous as her parents. But she couldn't lie. She wanted the flashing lights and fun times with her friends—the slackers!

Neither one answered her text. She started to call them but… Ugh!

"What are you up to?"

Starr's heart pumped in surprise as she looked at her father and Jordan standing in the doorway. "Um, just ummm… doing homework. It's real quiet in here."

Her father looked down at his diamond-encrusted watch. "Okay, well, we gotta go. Alicia and Swizz are on the way. They have a song for your moms," her dad said, backing out of the studio.

Starr smiled and nodded, ever conscious of Jordan's eyes on her. The sadness she saw tugged at her heart, but she pushed it aside. Her mama always warned her that when you lie down with dogs, you get up with fleas.

"I'm coming, Mr. Lester," Jordan said before stepping into the room.

Starr held her notepad to her chest as she eyed him.

My heart won't let go.

"We said enough in the bathroom…don't ya think?" she said under her breath.

Jordan shoved his hands into the pockets of his stiff black denims. He shrugged, moving over to the digital controls. "What are you recording?" he asked instead.

"Mind yours," she said, stepping over to brush his hand away from the control board. The feel of his hand was warm and she instantly pulled away.

His eyes dropped down to her retreating hand, before he

smiled and then hit the playback button. The first strains of the track filled the air. Jordan nodded. "This is nice, real nice. Like this," he said, moving his fingers as if he was the one playing the notes on the piano.

Jordan began to sing a melody along with the music. The soulfulness of his voice was clear and Starr stood there watching him, completely and totally awestruck—starstruck, lovestruck and dumbstruck.

He turned and grabbed her hand, his thumb massaging circles against her index finger as he switched it up and sang a riff of her name while he looked into her eyes.

My heart won't let go, she thought.

Yes, it can and it will, Starr promised herself as she pulled her hand free, stepped back from him, and broke the eye hold.

"You're wrong about me," Jordan said, hitting the playback button.

"Really?" she said, forcing herself not to look away from his intense stare.

"Yup."

"Did you and Heather go out?" she asked.

Jordan looked up to the ceiling. "We kicked it a little bit," he admitted.

Starr stung.

"But I never went all the way with her, and I don't have a baby on the way, Starr," he insisted.

"Then why did she even take a pregnancy test?"

"Huh?" he asked, his cute face looking confused.

Starr sat her BlackBerry and notepad down. "If she

didn't even think she could be pregnant then why take the test?"

"Heather claims she never had sex—I know she never had any with me—and people were lying about her so she took the test to show them she wasn't pregnant, not to make sure she wasn't."

Starr shrugged. "It doesn't matter," she said.

"Why?" he asked.

"Because whatever you do is your business and what you're looking for is a girl to let you play all over their body. That's *not* me, and I'm okay with that."

"I know that, Starr," Jordan said.

She shook her head, raking her fingers through her bangs. "I just don't get why everybody is giving it up like church fans on a hot day," she said.

"You don't?" he asked in total disbelief.

Starr pierced him with her eyes. "No I don't what? Understand or give it up?"

Jordan smiled. "Understand."

She rolled her eyes. "I'm not that girl, Jordan," she stressed again.

"I know that, Starr," he stressed again.

She studied him with her eyes. "We're on two different levels," she said, the truth sinking in. "I think we should just stay friends. I'm not mad at you. You're not mad at me. We're just not meant for each other."

"Man, come on, Starr," Jordan said.

"Yo, Jordan, let's go." Her father's voice came over the intercom through the studios. "Time is money, young 'un."

"Starr."

"What, Jordan?"

The door to the studio opened. Rico, one of her dad's engineers, stuck his head inside. "Jordan, we need you ASAP."

Starr raised her hand and waved. "There's plenty of Heathers in the world but only one Starr."

Fourteen

Dionne

October 23@1:25pm | Mood: Deceptive

DIONNE yawned, which drew the curious stares of her classmates and her French teacher, Ms. Toussaint, who was Haitian. She immediately clamped her mouth shut.

"Il faut dormir la nuit et rester à l'écart du téléphone avec des petits garçons," Ms. Toussaint asked, her almond-shaped eyes twinkling.

The entire class burst into laughter. Dionne flushed in embarrassment. Her French teacher was right. She *was* sleepy from staying up all night on the phone.

It was nice talking to Hassan about everything and nothing. When it was just the two of them it was like Lauryn Hill and D'Angelo's "Nothing Even Matters."

"Nothing but you, nothing but you," Dionne sang in her head.

"Accorder une attention, Dionne," Ms. Toussaint chided Dionne, from her seat behind her desk at the front of the classroom.

Dionne nodded, making sure that she did pay attention,

or at least look like it. But that was hard for a girl to do when she was deep in the goodness of a first love. Sigh.

HASSAN
&
DIONNE
a e i o u
1 2 3 4 5
2 1 1 1 0
=3 3 4 5 5

Two pairs and a run of 3-4-5, Dionne thought with satisfaction, drawing hearts around the pairs at the childish game that could supposedly predict your future with a boy by adding up the vowels in both your names.

"Awww. *Dionne est dans l'amour.*"

Dionne froze and looked up to find her French teacher standing over her. All eleven pairs of eyes of her fellow students were on her at their teacher's announcement that that she was in love. EMBARRASSING.

"Répétez après moi," she said politely, in French as smooth as silk.

Dionne sank lower on her chair.

"Dionne aime Hassan."

"Dionne loves Hassan," the class said loudly, in unison.

Dionne dropped her head in shame, her cheeks felt warm.

"Dionne ne fait pas attention en classe."

"Dionne does not pay attention in class."

Dionne couldn't do anything but shake her head.

"Dionne doit se concentrer ou à l'échec."

"Dionne must focus or fail," the class chorused.

Her tall and regal teacher held up her hand, signaling the class was to pause. Everyone understood. "*Comprendre,* Dionne?" Ms. Toussaint asked, lightly placing her hand on Dionne's shoulder.

Dionne nodded. *"Oui, mademoiselle. Je comprends."*

The school bell sounded and the teacher moved toward her desk, giving out their homework instruction in French. Dionne quickly gathered up her things and left class, avoiding her teacher's watchful eye.

"Who's Hassan?"

Dionne let out a dramatic gasp worthy of an MTV Movie Award as she turned to find Starr leaning against the wall of the hallway with her books in her hand.

"Heyyyy, Starr," she said, her voice filled with a nervous—and slightly guilty—tremor.

Starr eyed her strangely. "Who's Hassan?" she asked again.

Dionne thought quick. Tell the truth or a lie? She shrugged nonchalantly as they began walking down the crowded halls. "Some cute guy who works for my dad, but he's waaaay too old for me."

"Like Marisol's fascination with Trey Songz," Starr said.

"Definitely," Dionne lied.

She would like nothing better than for her besties to meet Hassan, but how long before her secret was revealed? And how would Hassan feel being the only kid in the group without unlimited funds to do whatever, whenever, wherever?

"My parents just texted me. They're having a huge Halloween masquerade ball for charity," Starr said, moving up the hall oblivious to whether someone might step into her path.

Dionne smiled so big that all her teeth showed. She loved, loved, loved parties at the Lesters'. They took over-the-top to a whole 'nother level.

"Arc you and Eric going to do one of those 'Excuse me while I barf' couple costumes?" Starr asked.

Dionne frowned. "Me and Eric?" she asked, as she spied a senior student sliding a package of cigarettes into his book bag out of the corner of her eye. *What kid wanted chimney lungs?* she thought.

"That's your boo you're always texting and on the phone with, right?"

Dionne opened her mouth. "Uhm...yeah," she lied again, thinking her tongue was going to be good and bumpy by the end of the school day if she kept it up.

Her mind was so busy trying to cover her tracks that she almost missed Jordan and Starr passing each other in the hall with puppy-dog eyes. "What's with the sad face?" she asked.

Marisol came down the adjoining hall. "Hey, clique," she said sweetly, her eyes bright.

"I told Jordan—like seriously—we could only be friends. Any delusions of JorStarr was such a done da-da," Starr admitted.

"Why?" Marisol asked, pouting her glossy lips as she reached across Dionne to rub Starr's hand.

"We're like Usher and Chilli," Starr said. "In two different places in our life."

"Awww," Dionne and Marisol said in unison.

Star shrugged. "An-y-way I will be going solo to the masquerade ball," she said.

"Then I'll be solo, too," Dionne said, actually grateful for the out.

They both turned to Marisol, who immediately looked frustrated. "Me three," she said, resigned and not at all looking happy about it.

Ding-dong.

Starr and Marisol looked down at Dionne's phone.

"My new text tone," she said, turning to head up the stairs. "See y'all after school."

The three friends went their separate ways to their last-period classes. Dionne paused before the door to the class to open her text she saw was from her mom.

Have fun at Starr's and your dad's this weekend.

Dionne texted back "okay" and walked into class with her mind on Hassan, and not caught up in finding a new house. She wanted to take Hassan to the party. She wanted to wear a sickeningly cute couple costume: Romeo and Juliet, Cole and Sasha, Angelina and Brad, Bonnie and Clyde. Whatever. It would have been big-time with Hassan at her side.

Dionne mentally sighed as she pulled her netbook from

her messenger bag. She noticed her cell vibrating away. Careful not to take it out, she set the bag in her lap and scrolled through the menu. She had a new Google alert.

She'd set up alerts for any and everything that truly interested her—mostly her dad and herself. Being the child of a celebrity meant that she was mentioned in plenty of entertainment e-zines and sites.

This one was a blog post about her dad:

Multiplatinum hip-hop star Lahron the Don to wed video-vixen Candylixxxious.

Dionne's mouth fell open. "What!" she snapped.

It nearly dropped to the floor when she saw a picture of her dad posed beside his tricked-out black-on-black Denali with Candylixxxious leaning against him in a thong bikini with his hands on the curve of her back, just above one of the biggest butts Dionne had ever seen. She didn't even bother to read the story as she shot a text to her dad.

R u getting married???!! :(

Dionne could barely keep her focus in class as she waited for him to hit her back. She sighed.

Starr thought she was still "talking to" Eric.

She and Marisol still hadn't figured out how to tell Starr that nails on a chalkboard miked through a PA system sounded better than her singing.

Her mom was dragging her feet in picking out a house.

Her dad was dating/marrying/doinggodknowswhat with

a video vixen. And to top it all off, every day her lies were getting harder and harder to keep up with.

Life = DRAMA.

fifteen

Marisol

October 23@3:43 p.m. | Mood: Supportive

"Let's go, la-dies," Marisol insisted as she eyed Starr and Dionne giggling over something on the internet. She was already dressed and ready to start practicing their routine.

Starr looked over from her desk. "What are you rushing for?" she asked, still dressed in the outfit she wore to school.

Because I am outta here at six to go see my baby's game. Marisol sighed as she paced half the length of Starr's bedroom—back and forth, back and forth. She tapped her foot with her arms crossed over her chest. "I'm ready to get started," she insisted.

Dionne grabbed her mini-duffel and headed for the bathroom. "I'm changing, Marisol. I'm changing."

"Good."

Starr eyed her as she cruised the net. "Actually I'm glad you're all ready to go. It's hard being the only one to grind so hard."

Marisol bit her lip to keep from telling her that she wished

Starr's attempts at singing would grind to a halt. "I'm just ready to practice."

They both looked at the door as Starr's doorbell chimed. Marisol went back to pacing and Starr used her remote to turn her TV to her surveillance camera.

"What in the heck is she doing here?"

Marisol turned and eyed the pretty redhead on the screen. "Who is she?" she asked.

"Natalee Livingston," Starr said, turning her attention back to the computer. "Her dad and my dad are in business together, and my mom and her mom want us to be besties. Picture that happening."

Marisol's eyes went from the TV to the door to Starr and back again. TV. Starr. Door. "Aren't you going to let her in?" she asked, watching Natalee examine her nails.

"I didn't invite her," Starr said.

Marisol's eyes widened. "That is so rude, Starr. Let the girl in," she said, crossing the floor to pull the door open.

"Hi," she said, her voice husky. "I'm Natalee."

Marisol stepped back just as Dionne stepped out of the bathroom in her practice gear: shorts, tank top and long colorful socks. "I'm Marisol and that's Rainbow Brite aka Dionne," she said with a friendly smile.

"Ha-ha," Dionne drawled.

Natalee walked into the suite, looking casual chic in a camel-colored ostrich-skin leather jacket with a matching cashmere-and-silk blend asymmetrical sweater and velvet straight-leg pants. Long, gold chains pulled it all together. The color was phenomenal with her deep reddish-auburn hair. "Hey, Starr," she said.

Starr barely raised her hand in a wave.

Marisol rolled her eyes. "Love, love, love that outfit."

Natalee smiled. "Thanks. I just love Gucci," she said.

"So does Starr," Dionne said from her spot on the floor as she pulled on her sneakers.

Marisol's eyebrows shot up as Starr whipped around to shoot Dionne a vicious dagger with her eyes as Starr made her way into her walk-in closet. "Starr, can you get dressed now, please?" she said, remembering her date with her dimpled football player, Percy.

She grabbed her cell phone from her pocketbook to text him.

C u @ the game

"There goes my baby..."

Marisol opened her text.

Wear the T-shirt I got u. U r my good luck charm.

Her smile was brighter than the Friday night lights of the football field.

:)

"There goes my baby," Natalee sang low in her throat as she flipped through a magazine.

Marisol's eyes shot in Natalee's direction, surprised by the pure *blue-eyed soul* that came from her mouth.

"Loving everything you do..."

She looked at Dionne. Dionne looked at her. They gave each other the meaningful eye like "Did you hear that?"

"Oh my God, your voice is off the chain," Dionne said, pulling her hair up into a ponytail.

Natalee looked up in surprise. "Me?" she asked, pointing to herself with a gold-tipped finger.

"Sí," Marisol said.

"Thanks," she said. "My dad's always telling me to stop singing so much."

"You like R&B?" Dionne asked.

Natalee nodded. "I like all kinds of music," she said.

Marisol gave Dionne another meaningful stare before she turned to Natalee with a huge Kool-Aid grin. "You sound…"

"Black," Dionne said bluntly.

"Soulful," Marisol finished.

Natalee removed her leather jacket. "Do you two go to Pace, too?" she asked, changing the subject.

"Yeah, sure," Marisol said dismissively with a wave of her light brown hand. "Do you know any Mary J. Blige?"

Natalee nodded, her glossy curls brushing against her face. "Love her *My Life* CD."

"Me, too," Dionne and Marisol said in unison.

They all laughed.

"Life can be only what you make it," Natalee sang, closing her eyes and tilting her head back as she sang from her soul.

Marisol felt goose bumps. A white girl with soul was not unheard-of: Amy Winehouse, Joss Stone, Teena Marie.

The closet door opened and Starr stepped out in her

bra and shorts. "What was that?" she asked. "Who was that?"

"We have a mini Amy Winehouse in the building," Dionne said.

Starr's eyes shifted to Natalee. "It sounded okay," she said, as she pulled a T-shirt on.

"O-kay? Okay? The girl can *saaang,*" Dionne said. "Seriously."

"You should join our group," Marisol offered.

"Now that's what's up," Dionne said, excited.

"A singing group?" Natalee asked.

"No!" Starr belted.

Marisol, Dionne and Natalee turned their heads toward her.

Starr smiled. "We already have everything planned for just the three of us," she said.

"I vote that she's in," Marisol said, thinking it was the perfect solution for Starr's lackluster vocals. "All in favor?"

Dionne's hand shot up.

Marisol clapped. "We can fit her in. It's not too late."

"Can I talk to you two?" Starr said, turning to walk into her theater room.

Marisol and Dionne looked at each other long and hard before they followed her. Starr was pacing. Hard.

"I cannot believe you two have the audacity to invite somebody into *my* group," she snapped, her eyes flashing.

"But she's good, Starr," Marisol insisted.

"Unlike you, I won't be receiving help for my part in the group."

Huh? Say what? "What does that mean?"

Starr shrugged. "Our new choreographer starts today," she said, looking Marisol square in the eye.

"Uh-oh," Dionne said from behind.

"That's cool," Marisol said, turning to leave the room.

"I really don't want to be in a singing group," Natalee said to her, almost sounding bored with the whole idea as she flipped the page of the magazine.

"Smart girl," Marisol said.

Starr and Dionne walked back in the room. "Okay, Natalee, we're about to practice sooooo..."

Natalee smiled a little. "I understand. I'll just go find my mother."

The smile Starr gave her was cold.

Marisol eyed her friend. "Starr, you really should let her sing since you—"

"Hey, so let's practice," Dionne said, obviously cutting Marisol off.

Humph. She's so tone-deaf she probably thinks Natalee is the one who sounds terrible! Marisol thought.

Marisol watched their new choreographer, Eli, carefully as he showed them a series of steps for the chorus of the song. She was determined to nail it. Starr thought she wasn't skilled enough to come up with their routines. Fine. Whatevs. Still, she was going to show them she was the best dancer in the group—if Starr didn't already know.

"Okay, girls," Eli said, his wrists as loose as his hips.

Marisol took her spot to the left of Starr, who was front and center.

The music filled the dance studio.

"Five, four, three, two, one… Get it!"

Marisol kept her eyes locked on her reflection in the mirror as she gave the dance her all. Fire was in her eyes. Skills were in her dance steps. Rhythm was in her hips.

She didn't even notice that Dionne and Starr faltered and that she was dancing through the routine alone until she hit her final pose with her hand up high in the air and her legs spread wide.

"Girl, you are fierce," Eli said, walking up to Marisol as she finally relaxed her pose. "I am scared of you, chica!"

Marisol smiled as her chest heaved and she gasped in large breaths. "Thank you."

"Girl, you make me say J-Who?" he joked.

Marisol beamed.

Dionne looked on proudly.

Starr looked begrudgingly impressed.

"Okay, gotta go," she said, turning to walk over to the benches.

"You're not staying?" Starr asked.

Marisol grabbed her duffel. "Percy has a game," she said.

"Eli, is that everything you were working on today?" she asked, checking her watch. *My driver should be outside.*

"Yes and you nailed it," he said.

Marisol nodded, threw up a deuce, and exited Starr's suite.

Marisol took in everything around Pace Academy's football field. It was the first time she'd ever been to a game, and she couldn't wait for Percy and the rest of the team to take the field.

She was big-time excited when they began to announce the players. She yelled and clapped the loudest when Percy's name was called. When he looked up into the stands to find her, she waved and gave him her best smile.

Did she feel bad about missing practice and the sleepover? Nope. Starr had hurt her feelings by dropping her as the choreographer even though she didn't show it.

"Girl, you are fierce!"

She remembered Eli's compliment. That mattered more to her, because dance was her thing. Plus, she was beginning to think that her claim to fame had nothing to do with music and the Go Gettas.

sixteen

Starr
October 25@1:00 p.m. | Mood: Relaxed

The Lester household was filled with activity as everyone made last-minute preparations for the Halloween party—more like extravaganza.

Starr was stressed about getting a costume designed for the party, working overtime on the Go Gettas, preparing for the talent show and keeping up with her schoolwork.

To top it all off, she was missing Jordan and annoyed by the ever-growing presence of Natalee "I think I'm Mary J. Blige" Livingston in her life.

"You're tense, Starr," Inga said, putting more pressure on Starr's thin shoulders as she gave her a massage.

The thought of Natalee made Starr tense—big-time. That night at the Livingstons' house had only confirmed what Starr already knew—Natalee's life was fabulous, maybe even more so than her own. Natalee's gorgeously styled suite of rooms with a loft and a secret door leading to a passageway to the home's elaborate games room in the basement. Her closet was exactly like Mariah's New York penthouse walk-in closet. Of course, Natalee was nice enough in that laid-back, bored kind of way that might make a less secure person feel like a fifth wheel. But there was room for only one star in Starr's world. And that was why she had tried her best to downplay Pace Academy to Natalee, who was looking for a broader social life. Natalee Livingston, the stylish white girl with black-girl flavor at *her* school—heck no!

"Relax, Miss Starr," Inga encouraged.

Starr tried to force herself to chill out, but it was easier said than done.

As soon as the massage was over, Starr wrapped a white Egyptian cotton bath sheet around her body. Inga packed away the massage table and quietly made her exit. Starr looked up as her assistant, Olivia, passed her a fuchsia terrycloth robe. "Thanks," Starr said, standing in her bare feet to wrap the robe around herself, letting the bath sheet drop to the floor of her bedroom suite.

Olivia was an intern at TopStarr Records and also worked as Starr's part-time, on-call personal assistant. She adjusted her black-rimmed glasses on her face and opened a leather portfolio.

"Fiyah will be arriving next weekend. I have him booked in a deluxe suite at the Hilton. I emailed him the lyrics you forwarded me and he should get back to us tomorrow with any suggestions," Olivia said.

Starr nodded as she moved to take her seat at her desk.

"The stylist has agreed to meet the Go Gettas here the day of the talent show to do makeup and get you all dressed," she continued.

"She's coming to the talent show, right?" Starr asked, momentarily taking her eyes off her Facebook account.

Olivia nodded and scratched something on her portfolio. "Yes, to help you with the performance outfits you approved."

Starr logged out of Facebook and logged into her Twitter account.

"Eli is confirmed to practice here every Friday until the night of the talent show."

Starr clicked on Jordan's profile page.

JORDAN_JACKSON: ya boy is on Ustream. Holla at me!!!!

She clicked the link, wondering why she was torturing herself. "Maybe he's not on anymore."

"You said something, Starr?" Olivia asked.

She shook her head as Jordan's image filled the screen. Her eyes soaked him in as she ignored the hundreds of girls telling him how cute he was and how they wanted to marry him and kiss him.

"Feeling completely misunderstood. But y'all know how that is, right?" he said, as he gave his lips a lick.

"And your mom's stylist is coming over today with everyone's costumes."

"Have you ever been feeling someone who wasn't feeling you?" he asked.

"Starr. Starr?"

She looked away from Jordan as he began to sing. "Huh?"

"I'm still working on the other items you requested for the stage show," Olivia said, handing her the cup of hot water with lemon and honey that Starr requested. "Mimi said be careful. It's hot."

Starr was so caught up with Jordan, who she saw was bare-chested, that she didn't notice that Mimi had come into her room and left.

"Is that Jordan?" Olivia asked, standing next to Starr's fuchsia leather chair.

"Yup."

"The girls love them some Jordan," Olivia said, before turning to walk away.

Starr looked at his viewer count as the numbers increased by the second and the chat room filled with girls trying to get his attention. How could she compete with that?

She closed her computer just as her bedroom door opened. Her mother walked in. Starr smiled. Her mom was so cool, so fly, so laid-back, so fabulous.

"Wanted to check on my baby girl," she said, looking fab in gray cashmere lounge pants, a white Lycra tank top and a turquoise wrap sweater that draped open. Her hair was in a loose topknot and five-carat platinum diamond studs were on her lobes.

"How's the album coming?" Starr asked, once Olivia had left the room.

"Good," Sasha said. "I'm ready to get back and do my thing, especially performing on stage. I love it."

Maybe the Go Gettas could open up for Sasha's world tour! Starr thought, adding it to her to-do list.

Starr enjoyed the attention. Her parents were always on

the go and she lived for the rare moments they carved out for family time. She started to tell her about the talent show but she held back. First she wanted to make sure the Go Gettas ish was on point.

"What did you have Olivia doing for you?" Sasha asked.

"Some things for school," she said, intentionally being vague. She had already sworn Olivia to secrecy.

"How's school going?" her mother asked, reaching for a rhinestone-covered brush.

"Good. I got an A on my English test," Starr said.

"You always get good grades, but then Pace is a good school, a *really* good school…certainly not a place with gang violence and sexual assaults and teachers who smoke weed with the students."

Uh-oh.

"Starr, why in the hell did you try to discourage Natalee from going to Pace? Did you say all those things?" Sasha asked, sitting down on the foot of her daughter's bed and crossing her legs.

Starr kept her eyes locked on her mother's painted toenails as she shrugged.

"Look at me, Starr," her mother said in a no-nonsense voice that she rarely used.

Starr obeyed. "But, Ma, why does she have go to Pace?"

Sasha's face became incredulous. "Because she wants to, Starr. You can't dictate the comings and goings at Pace. You're trippin', little girl."

Starr pouted. "I have friends. I have a life. Why are you

forcing this girl on me? When did I become the welcome committee for lonely teens?"

Sasha eyed her daughter for a long time as her foot swung up and down like she was charging something up with static electricity. "People say we spoil you and give you too much. They say we're raising mini-monsters. They say we aren't giving you real values because we give you so many material things."

Starr shifted her eyes away from her mom's.

"I thought we had a good balance. I thought we were doing right by you and your brothers, letting you enjoy everything we *worked* hard to get." Sasha stood up. "Knowing you would lie to someone to get your way, Starr, makes me wonder if we were wrong."

Starr said nothing and her mother turned and walked out of the suite, leaving behind a room filled with disappointment.

seventeen

Dionne

October 28@7:35 p.m. | Mood: Happy

DIONNE was more than a little stressed. Even though Marisol and Starr were putting up a big-time front at being cool with each other, the tension was thick as gravy. It was getting so bad that she was glad to be out of the tug-of-war between them and go back home to Newark every day.

Starr said Marisol was acting like she wasn't used to having a boyfriend.

Marisol said Starr was ego tripping and way too judgmental when she couldn't sing.

She usually pleaded the fifth and tried to stay out of it.

In truth, Dionne thought Starr was wrong to drop Marisol as their choreographer without telling her. And she understood why asking Natalee to be a singer in the group had hurt Starr's feelings.

Other than that drama, Dionne was actually excited about the group. She liked the tracks. She loved the outfits and was pumped about the choreography—Marisol's and Eli's. But she also just couldn't see anyone taking them seriously with Starr as the lead vocalist—not at all.

They really and truly needed Natalee.

But Starr would never admit it and Dionne didn't think she would ever have the heart to tell her. But someone had to…before the talent show.

Dionne sighed as she looked down at the time on her BlackBerry. Hassan had football practice Monday through Thursday and she didn't get to see him until eight. Usually, he would come over and they'd chill while he did his homework.

"Ma," Dionne yelled from the living-room window seat, where she was pretending to read some random book while waiting for Hassan.

"What?" Risha called back, the smell of fried chicken in the air.

"You haven't picked out a house yet?" she asked.

"Between you and your daddy I'm gonna scream," Risha said, walking into the living room.

"Just asking, Ma."

Risha eyed the window. "Sitting there waiting on your little boo ain't gonna bring him here sooner," she said, with a playful twist of her mouth.

Dionne just buried her head in the book.

"And what does Hassan think about you moving? Not that it matters," she stressed. "I'm just curious."

"We're not boyfriend and girlfriend," Dionne said.

"As much as he's been hangin' around here I thought I was going to hear wedding bells as soon as you two graduate," Risha quipped.

"You're so funny, Ma, I forgot to laugh."

Risha cocked her head to the side. "I'll let that slide

because I can tell something's bothering you. Is it about that music group? Do I have to be the Sonja to your Brandy or the Jonetta to your Usher?"

Dionne smiled, knowing Risha Hunt would be as good as those momagers combined, plus some. "I'm good," she said.

"Sure?"

"A-plus."

"Somebody at work told me that your daddy's getting married," she said. "And don't act like you don't know because mother knows all about your Google alerts and daily blog reads."

Dionne winced at an image of Candylixxxious's *ginormous* behind. "Is that his type?" she asked.

Risha stood up and looked down at her own buttocks. "It wasn't sixteen years ago," she quipped. "I guess more money, more booty."

"O-kay," Dionne agreed, glad that she wasn't the piece of thong caught in Candylixxxious's behind. "But he said that's a lie. They went out, but no haps on the walk down the aisle."

"Did you finish your rhyme?" she asked.

Dionne shrugged. "Yeah, Daddy helped me with it. He claims my flow is sick," she bragged, dancing in her chair and snapping her fingers.

"Let me see for myself. I grew up on hip-hop," she joked, like she was still fifteen and back in the 1980s.

"Let me tighten it up first. Okay?"

Ding-dong.

"Mr. Lover-Lover is here." Risha stood up and walked back into the kitchen.

Dionne was excited as she buzzed him in. She stood in the doorway and listened to the sound of his feet on the steps.

And then it kinda hit her that her crush—her very first crush—was crushing on her just as hard. *Life is good.*

Hassan smiled when he saw her. "Hey, are we going to the big Halloween party at Cole Lester's?" he asked as soon as he walked in the house.

Dionne's stomach dropped.

"Hey, Ms. Hunt," he called out.

"Hi, Hassan," she called back.

Dionne turned all the lights on. "Party?" she asked.

"Yeah, it's all over the blogs. The kids were talking about it at school." Hassan dug his schoolbooks out of his book bag once he had settled his tall athletic frame. He wore a hoodie over his football jersey and oversize basketball shorts and Jordans.

"I think it's for adults," she told him, as she discovered that lying was becoming easier and easier.

Hassan looked disappointed. "That's cool. There's a Halloween party at Westside and we can just go to that," he offered.

Oh, crap! Miss the party? No way. "Sounds like a plan," she said, turning to walk into the kitchen.

"Liar, liar," her mother said under her breath.

Dionne ignored her and grabbed a can of soda from the fridge. Of course her mom knew she was lying. They'd already rented her costume. Dionne sat the soda can next to

Hassan and then plopped down onto the sofa. She frowned as she felt something pressing into her bottom. She stood and looked down. It was a gold cardboard jewelry box.

Her eyes got big as she looked at Hassan pretending like he was focused on his math homework.

Playing along, she said nothing else and opened the box. She gasped in pleasure at the three gold bangles nestled in the square of white foamy cushion.

Dionne slid them over her slender hand onto her wrist before she turned and hugged Hassan's sweaty neck. "Thank you, Hassan. They're sooooo cute," she sighed, thinking the sweat from his football practice workout smelled better than the most expensive cologne.

As her heart beat faster, she allowed herself to inhale deeply of the scent of sweat and the faint remnants of some cologne.

"I know they ain't as nice as the ones you lost when you got robbed, but I thought you'd like 'em," he said, leaning back to look up at her.

Dionne's face was just above his. Their eyes met. She brought her hand up to the side of his face as he raised his chin and pressed his mouth to hers. It felt like a scene out of a movie. Dionne sighed as he lightly touched her lips with his tongue.

Chills…up and down my spine…

"You my girl?" he asked huskily, his minty-fresh breath breezing against her mouth.

Wow.

Dionne raised her head and nodded. Hassan snuck one last soft peck before he placed his hands on her hips and pushed her back toward her seat on the sofa. "Your moms don't play," he whispered to her as he lifted his book bag into his lap to search for something.

"Y'all mighty quiet up there," Risha called from the kitchen or wherever she was ear hustling.

He gave Dionne a comical look. "See!"

As Dionne opened her laptop and logged onto her computer science assignment, she tried to quell the guilt she felt. Hassan was *that* dude—cute, funny and completely fly. And she knew he liked her. He didn't hide it all. And with most guys so busy being cool and all swagged out, it was big-time nice to find one who let a girl know how he felt. The last thing he deserved was someone lying to him and being ashamed of him.

Dionne bit her lips, ignoring the taste of the lip gloss as she looked down at the bangles he'd bought her.

Her heart ached for him and for herself, because her grandmother always said, "What is done in the dark comes to the light." And when the lights came on, Dionne knew Hassan might not be there.

eighteen

Marisol

October 29@7:00 p.m.| Mood: Sad :(

"YOUR mother is a beautiful woman."

Marisol was leaning in the doorway of their living room looking on with pride as her mother was being interviewed for a feature in *Latina* magazine. She looked behind her, surprised to see her father standing there as well. Like her mother, Marisol wore all-white with bold turquoise jewelry.

"Dentro y por fuera," she said softly, as she turned back to her mother and the interviewer.

"*Sí,* you are right, Marisol. She is beautiful inside and out," her father agreed, looking handsome in a charcoal-gray suede blazer, matching silk shirt and dark rinse denims with polished square-toe shoes.

Even Carlos was nicely dressed in a suit—and that dumb cap—somewhere around the house, ready to take a family photo to accompany the article. Her mother would not settle for anything else but a picture of her family.

"As the wife of a celebrity athlete you could easily spend

your days shopping, but instead you put in a lot of hours at many of the charities that you support. Why is that?"

Yasmine smiled and nodded in agreement. "In this economy, I am very aware of how fortunate my family is because my husband is a famous athlete," she said, speaking more slowly than usual, so that her accent was less pronounced. "I feel that it afforded me a wonderful opportunity to do so much by contributing time and money for those less fortunate and in need. It's a blessing that I want to share."

Marisol knew her mother attended charity events and donated plenty of money to several organizations. But as she continued to listen to the interview, she became aware of all the contributions her mother had made—scholarships, working to open a shelter for victims of domestic abuse, donating a large sum to help fund a children's burn unit in a low-income neighborhood. Her mother's diligent work for more than a dozen charities involving women and children or health-related causes was finally being recognized.

"There goes my baby..."

Marisol stepped back from the doorway and answered the incoming call. She didn't miss the look on her father's face so she kept walking toward the kitchen to get some privacy.

"Hello," she said, already smiling.

Suddenly the phone was taken from her hand and Marisol turned around to see her father with her phone. *Oh Dios!*

"Who is this?" he asked in clipped tones, his eyes on Marisol.

"Daddy, no," she begged, horribly embarrassed as she stepped forward to take it back.

Her father held up his hand. "And why are you calling my daughter?"

Marisol turned and pressed the entire side of her face to the marble counter on the kitchen island.

"And you go to Pace?" Alex asked.

With each question Marisol died just a little.

"Well, Percy, do you think it is appropriate to be the friend of a man's daughter and not have the respect to come and meet her father?"

Marisol unstuck her face from the marble as her eyes got big as dollar coins.

"Good, then until you learn to put the first step back in front of the second—and not the other way around—do not call my daughter's phone."

Click.

Her father handed her the phone and Marisol reached for it.

"This *friend* that is a boy, is he your boyfriend?" he asked, sliding his hands into the pocket of his denims.

Marisol shook her head. She already knew an official *boyfriend* was a no-no until she was sixteen. "Just a friend, Papi," she said.

"You are not to talk to him again until after I talk to your mother about this tonight. Clear?"

Marisol knew from the look in her father's eyes that he meant business. *"Sí,* Papi."

He wrapped his arm around her shoulder as they walked back to the formal living room. *Still,* Marisol thought, *he didn't say anything about texting!*

★ ★ ★

Marisol couldn't wait to be alone in her room.

She was already putting her phone on vibrate and texting Percy before the door closed behind her good.

Sorry 4 that earlier. Dad is trippin hard.

Bzzz.

No problem. IMU.

Bzzz.

Aww. IMU2.

Marisol set her phone down and flopped back onto her bed. She turned her head and eyed her newly dry-cleaned costume hanging on the clothes rack she used to hang the outfits she picked out for school the night before.

Between Starr firing her as the choreographer and the two of them barely being cordial since then, Marisol considered not even going to party at all, especially since they'd made the dumb pact not to bring dates because Starr didn't have one. Ugh! Double ugh!

Marisol flopped over onto her stomach as she lay across her bed. Outside of what little time they saw each during school and very briefly after school before he went to football practice, Marisol hardly saw Percy at all. It wasn't like she could tell her parents she was going out to the movies with a boy. No haps.

It would have been so cool to chill with him at the party. Take pictures. Maybe even share that first kiss.

She'd given the girls her word though.

Still, weren't they wrong to even ask her to give her word?

Knock-knock.

"What, *vato?*" she asked, knowing it was Carlos.

The door opened and he stuck his curly head in. "Mommy and Daddy want you," he said.

Marisol rolled off the bed and kicked off her heels, deciding to leave her phone behind before her father caught on that she was texting Percy.

Her brother ran ahead of her down the hall and the staircase making noises like he was in a NASCAR race. Marisol took her time, still weighing her options: hanging out with her girls or chilling with Percy.

Decisions, decisions…

Before she was halfway down the stairs, she heard the familiar loudness and laughter of her extended family. The rooms downstairs were filled to capacity.

Everyone must have arrived around the same time because Marisol knew when she went up the stairs there was no one else but the immediate family.

She made the rounds, kissing, hugging and being spun around by grandparents, aunts, uncles and older cousins. The sound of rapid-fire Spanish filled the air and soon the aroma of traditional Spanish food mingled with it.

Her eyes searched for her father and found him sparring playfully with Carlos while he talked to his darker-skinned brother Miguel. Her mother was lying on the chaise by the patio doors—which was unusual for someone who took being hostess very seriously.

Marisol was heading her mother's way to check on her when she saw her father move to her mother's side. He helped his wife to her feet and then motioned for both Marisol and Carlos to join them.

Curious, Marisol moved toward them, wishing she had known they were having guests so that she would have put on some shoes.

"Yasmine and I wanted to have the family around us as we share some exciting news about our family," Alex said, placing his free hand atop her brother's head.

The chef strolled into the room pushing a cart with a huge and colorful cake in the shape of a crib.

The entire room gasped.

"Un bebé?" some asked softly.

"Sí. Sí. Un bebé," her mother said with a smile.

Marisol stood there staring at the cake as all their relatives surged forward to congratulate them. She was just starting to figure it out. As much as she loved her little *hermano,* Carlos, he could be a real pain with little effort. *What if it's two against one?* she wondered. *Our entire wing of the house will smell like Cheez Doodles and onions!* Marisol had to fight the urge to run across the room screaming like a banshee, kicking and stomping the cake with her feet.

nineteen

Starr
October 31@9:00 p.m.| Mood: Spooky

The sound of music filtered upstairs to Starr's bedroom as her mom's makeup artist finished with a few last-minute touch-ups to her makeup. When the mirror was pushed into her hands she was excited to see her final transformation into Tinkerbell.

The exaggerated glitter and colorful eye makeup worked perfectly with her bangs and loose top. Starr hopped down off the makeup chair and studied her image in the full-length mirror. The strapless, green sequined dress was a more refined rendition of the fairy-tale character's look with a corset and wide ballerina tutu, even down to the wings attached to the costume at her shoulder blades. A shimmer of glitter was lightly sprinkled over her entire body. She even had the satin green slippers with a furry ball on each one.

"Perfect," Starr said, turning this way and that in the mirror.

The only thing that didn't feel right was not having Marisol and Dionne there with her. In the past, the girls would have brought their costumes with them and stayed the night, talking about the upcoming party. They would have gotten their hair done together and gotten their makeup done together. And gotten dressed to go down to the party together.

Dionne decided to come with her dad, and Marisol? Starr wasn't even sure she was still coming. She tried to shrug it off like she didn't care, but she did.

Clutching her magic wand, Starr followed the glam squad to her mother's room where she was awaiting final touches to her Cleopatra makeup. Her dad was going as Egyptian pharaoh King Tut.

"Sash, baby, you got to hurry or we'll miss our own red carpet," Cole Lester said.

Starr tapped her father's broad shoulder and he turned, chomping on a cigar that looked out of place with his long white tunic, ornate sash, collar and armbands. His headpiece was gold. The only thing he lacked was the heavy kohl liner around his eyes.

"Whaddup, Tinkerbell?" he said, pinching her glitter-dusted cheek.

"What's the haps, King Tut?" Starr joked.

"Okay, I'm ready," Sasha said.

Starr and her dad turned toward her. "Wow, Mommy, you look good," Star said, saying a quick prayer that when she finally began to fill out she would inherit her mother's hourglass figure.

The costume was real sexy with a white halter top trimmed in gold and low slung skirt that only fell mid-thigh. The long, gold-trimmed cape flowed to the floor.

The ornate gold and turquoise collar and belt highlighted the glow of her caramel complexion. She wore a Cleopatra bob with a matching headpiece with thick kohl eyeliner embellished with rhinestones around her eyes.

"You like, my king?" she asked her husband with a flirtatious smile.

Cole nodded. "I like, my queen."

Starr sighed heavily as they kissed. She hated when her parents acted like horny teenagers. "Party downstairs! Red carpet! People waiting on us! Gotta go!" Starr said, grabbing their arms and pulling them to the door.

When my parents throw a party, they throw a party, she thought, holding her bejeweled Venetian-like mask up to her face as she moved around the crowded dance floor as "Ghostbusters" blared through the sound system.

The Lester mansion had been completely transformed into three different spaces. Their guests had to enter through a long, winding tent decorated as a haunted house, with an actor jumping out from behind a curtain to scare everyone who entered. As they entered, guests were greeted by actors in elaborately decorated zombie costumes, who served hors d'oeuvres, alcoholic and nonalcoholic beverages.

As they entered the next area, it was decorated with round, black, tablecloth-covered tables, with elaborate tree-like centerpieces draped in everything Halloween, from cobwebs to spiders. The darkness of the room was broken up by swirling orange strobe lights that created eerie-looking shadows that circled the walls, giving the space an elegant yet spooky feel that could only be described as Halloween couture.

The last space was the dance floor, which was decorated like a castle with an opulent decor.

Starr turned and looked toward the door, hoping to see Marisol or Dionne. Someone tapped her shoulder and she turned to find Natalee dressed in an elaborate glittery ball gown, with a huge crown and a star-topped wand.

"Who are you?" Starr snapped.

"Glenda, the Good Witch," she said.

Of course, Starr thought, with a stiff smile.

"This place is beautiful and creepy all at once," Natalee said, in a husky voice that could be heard over the sound of Rockwell's hit "Somebody's Watching Me."

Yes, kinda like you, Starr thought to herself.

Starr turned to keep her eye out for her girls—hard to do with nearly two hundred costume-wearing partygoers already filling the place.

"Why don't you like me?"

Starr frowned as she lowered her mask to look at Natalee. "Excuse me?" she said with attitude.

"Why don't you like me?" Natalee repeated, not flinching as Starr gave her a hard stare.

"I don't know what you're talking about. I don't have any feelings one way or the other about you, sweetie," Starr countered, feeling slightly uneasy at Natalee's directness.

Natalee flicked her glossy auburn spirals over her shoulder. "And you don't want to," she said.

Starr's shoulders tensed and she wished the music was a bit louder to drown her out. "Don't want to what?"

"Get to know me."

Starr locked eyes with Natalee. "I don't want to be forced to," she said truthfully.

Natalee nodded in understanding as she twirled her wand. "Me either, Starr," she said turning to walk away.

Starr eyed the top of the crown moving through crowd as it floated. She turned, dismissing the girl, but a tug of guilt hit her deep and she turned to search the crowd. Natalee was standing by her parents. Not dancing. Not talking with the other teens in the crowd. Just looking like a third wheel with her parents.

"I thought we had a good balance. I thought we were doing right by you and your brothers, letting you enjoy everything we worked hard to get. Knowing you would lie to someone to get your way, Starr, makes me wonder if we were wrong."

Ugh, Ma, Starr thought, hating that her mother's words clung to her like the infamous twins Poly and Ester. Starr headed off in Natalee's direction, sidestepping Wonder Woman, who was gyrating in front of Superman. She had to shoot the evil eye to a zombie pretending to come at her with outstretched arms as "Monster Mash" played loudly around them.

"Hello, Mr. and Mrs. Livingston," Starr said politely, keeping to herself that the choice to be Fred Flintstone and Wilma was dead-on, right down to his bare feet looking like they had been used to power a vehicle. Ew!

"Tinkerbell, you look beautiful," Mrs. Livingston gushed, the large pearls around her neck looking authentic.

"Thank you," Starr said, batting her long lashes as she

touched a button on her hips to make her wings flutter and light up.

"Well, look at that, Natalee," Mrs. Livingston cooed, clapping her hands.

The look on Natalee's face said "whoop dee-doo."

"My friends are staying over after the party and you're invited," Starr said.

Natalee arched an eyebrow. "Really?" she asked, sounding like Alicia Keys.

Starr stiffened. She wasn't quite sure whether her one-word response was sarcastic. "So let me know," she said, before turning to walk away.

She dismissed Natalee's reaction as she tried hard not to focus on how many Michael Jackson and Barack Obama costumes she saw as she made her way back to the front. Starr jumped in surprise as someone screamed from inside the haunted house tent. Several people with masks standing nearby laughed at her. Starr ignored them.

The lights flickered and the sound of eerie laughter filled the air, startling the crowd. Lights flashed around the stage as the curtains slowly opened and Michael Jackson's "Thriller" began to play.

The stage lights came on and the shadow of a dancing figure appeared behind a screen. The crowd applauded and whistled at the re-creation of Michael Jackson's signature dance moves.

Curious, Starr made her way to the front of the dance floor. "What is going on?" she asked herself as the figure jumped through the screen and posed.

Jordan.

Starr's heart pounded to see him in a costume like Michael Jackson's outfit from the "Thriller" video. Throughout his entire performance, her eyes were glued to him—his every move, his voice, his talent, his ability to connect with the audience, his intensity, everything. There was no mistaking that Jordan Jackson was going to be a huge star.

That thought made Starr happy and sad all at once.

twenty

Dionne
October 31@10:17 p.m. | Mood: Annoyed

DIONNE was big-time regretting her decision to stay at her dad's and ride with him to the costume party, masquerade ball—whatevs.

First, she had been big-time disappointed to find Candylixxxious comfortable as all get-out in the apartment in nothing but a pair of leggings and a wife beater that barely covered her gravity-defying breasts.

Next, discovering that her father was taking the star of more than twenty videos and an upcoming calendar to the party with them was mortifying.

Dionne eyed her dad's bedroom doors from her seat in front of the seventy-inch flat screen. No sight of them. Nothing but the faint smell of marijuana mingled with air freshener and incense sticks.

"Daddy!" Dionne yelled out sharply. "Let's go."

The door open and a thin trail of smoke escaped. Candylixxxious stepped out in a Playboy bunny outfit that didn't leave anything to anybody's imagination.

Dionne rolled her eyes.

"He's getting dressed now," she said, her voice soft and whispery and so completely unnatural.

"What were y'all doing all that time?" she snapped, big-time pissed off that Marisol texted her that she'd missed Jordan performing "Thriller."

Candylixxxious just laughed and laughed as she moved into the kitchen on four-inch heels.

"There goes my baby…"

Dionne picked up her BlackBerry. Hassan. "Hello," she said, frowning at the loud music and background noise.

"I wish you were here with me."

She stood up and moved across the large living room to the bay windows. Her reflection in the glass made it look like she was walking on air above the brightly lit New York City skyline. "Me, too," she said. "But my dad really wanted me to go with him."

Liar, liar, pants on fire.

"I understand. I just like hanging out with you, DiDi."

Her heart sank. *Awww.*

"I just wish my dad woulda let you come," she said, sticking to her lie as she focused on the view beyond the window, unable to stand the sight of her own reflection.

Pinocchio don't have ish on you, boo.

"Don't make me have to hurt no chick dancing up on you," she said. "I still got spies at Westside."

Hassan laughed. "If you really cared, you woulda been here with me," he joked.

That was so true.

"And don't get one of them preppy boys straight rocked, ya heard," he said.

Dionne smiled.

"Let's be out," her dad said from behind her.

Dionne frowned at the silk pajamas and housecoat he wore. "Daddy," she snapped. "Where is your costume?"

She pointed to her fedora, oversize rope chain, red and black Adidas tracksuit and sneakers without the laces. "You look nothing like the Run to my DMC," she said.

"Wow," Hassan said on the phone. "Hit me up later when y'all work that out."

She gladly hit the red phone icon.

"No, he's Hugh Hefner," Candylixxxious said, walking out of the kitchen with a bottle of Ciroc in her hand.

"Where are you going with *that?*" Dionne snapped.

"Dionne!" her father barked.

Dionne dropped down on the sofa. Pissed. So pissed.

"Apologize for being rude and disrespectful?" Lahron said, coming to stand over her.

Dionne was beyond hurt that her father picked his flavor of the month over her. Dionne fought the urge to tell Whackalixxxious to use her DDDs to float her behind out the door.

Candylixxxious shook her head. "I didn't know y'all had matching costumes, Dionne," she said, looking confused at Dionne's obvious anger at her.

Dionne shrugged. "Can we just go?" she asked.

"When you apologize and this is your last chance, Dionne," her dad said in a firm voice.

"Sorry," she said low in her throat, barely above a whisper, and not at all heartfelt.

For the entire trip to Starr's, Dionne said nothing from

her seat in the back. She even skipped the red carpet. Being seen as half of Run DMC with her rapper dad was cute. Standing in as a third wheel as DMC while Hef and Holly posed? Weird, whack and weak.

She accepted the huge tote bag of candy a ghoul handed her with a creepy grin showing off bloodstained teeth. Too authentic. Okay?

Dionne walked into the dark tent, hating that the door closed behind her, making the interior inky-black until lights flashed, momentarily revealing disfigured bodies and floating apparitions. As she continued to walk, eerie voices whispered to her, hands reached out for her, cobwebs clung to her face.

When the zombie-clown suddenly lunged at her, Dionne couldn't help but scream and run out of the tent. She knew it was all staged, but her heart was still beating like crazy.

"Finally!"

Dionne turned just in time for Tinkerbell to grab her wrist. "Starr?" she asked.

She nodded.

Dionne fumed. "You look all cute and current and I'm looking like a lesbian from the eighties!"

Starr stopped and turned to eye Dionne's costume with an apologetic shake of her head. "I'm sorry, bestie, but that costume went straight to the left because there is nothing right about it."

"Co-sign," Dionne agreed.

"Ew, my gosh."

Dionne followed Starr's line of vision directed at Candylixxxious, who was running out of the haunted tent emitting a little squeal, each of her breasts going up and down or left and right—but never in the same direction as the other.

"Welcome to my weekends at Daddy's," Dionne complained, still salty about the costume drama.

"Ooooh," Starr said, still eyeing the woman.

It was Dionne's turn to grab Starr's wrist. "Let's go find Marisol," she said.

"Okay, but let's go get you changed first. I have a really cute cowgirl costume from last Halloween," Starr said, leading the way through the crowd and out the doors of the ballroom.

"Thanks, Starr," Dionne said as they took the elevators up to the floor housing the bedrooms.

"I just hate that you missed Jordan's tribute to Michael Jackson…he completely killed it. Killllled it."

"Marisol said it was ballistic," Dionne said as Starr entered her security code and then opened the door.

Dionne ran into the back of her when Starr stopped. "Marisol's here already?" she asked.

Dionne nodded. "She and Percy are dressed as Bonnie and Clyde. I can't wait to see them," she said, already kicking off her Adidas sneakers.

"I thought we agreed no dates," Starr said, her voice sounding slightly annoyed as she walked into her closet and emerged moments later with the costume covered in a dry-cleaning plastic bag.

"Me, too, but it's okay," Dionne said. *Because if I could have brought Hassan I would have for sure,* she mused.

"She didn't even look for me," Starr said, sounding hurt.

Dionne stopped unzipping the jacket of her tracksuit. "I

think we all need to talk and to make the necessary apologies and not let forming the group mess up our friendship."

"Necessary apologies?"

Oh, boy. "Starr, you hired a new choreographer and didn't tell the girl. Come on now, Starr. That was messed up." Dionne eyed her. "Seriously, Starr!"

"I've put a lot of time, a lot of effort and a lot of money into this group, Dionne," she insisted, flopping down onto her bed. "If we are going to do this and do it right so that we do it big, then we all have to put in one hundred and ten percent."

"Listen, I want this, too. I've seen *Fame.* I've heard the speech. And yes, fame does cost but I don't want it to cost us our friendship. Do you?" Dionne asked.

Starr just stared at her colorful nails.

Dionne eyed her for a long time. The fact that Starr didn't answer her question definitely gave Dionne pause.

twenty-one

Marisol
October 31@10:40 p.m. | Mood: Excited

"GO, Percy! Go, Percy!" Marisol laughed as she watched his head dunk under the water again and come up with a shiny red apple in his teeth.

The people around them applauded, but no one clapped louder than Marisol as she gave him a hand towel to wipe his head and some of the water on the shoulders of his pin-striped suit.

Percy took the apple from his teeth and proudly presented it to Marisol, who looked like a couture-clad Bonnie Parker in her silver flapper dress and sequined headband and boa.

They left the games tent and headed for the dance floor as DJ Jazzy Jeff and the Fresh Prince's "Nightmare on Elm Street" filled the air. They started doing old-school dances.

Marisol was doing the Cabbage Patch when she saw Natalee standing on the edge of the dance floor by herself. She danced over to her and grabbed her wrist. "Come on," she said over the music, turning to pull the shy girl behind her.

Marisol started doing The Butt and Natalee laughed before she joined in. The three of them danced to the next five songs, enjoying the mix of Halloween-themed music with popular tracks. As Usher's "O.M.G." faded into the next song, Marisol had to fan herself as they finally walked off the dance floor.

"Let's go outside," Percy offered, taking Marisol's hand and waving for Natalee to follow.

"All that dancing made it hot in there," Marisol said, breathing in the chilly air.

"Thanks for coming to get me. I was getting a little bored not knowing anyone," Natalee said.

Marisol noticed the way the sound of Natalee's voice surprised Percy.

"That's nothing. You should hear her sing," she told him, accepting Percy's jacket to drape around her shoulders.

Percy eyed Natalee. "I don't listen to country or none of that Justin Bieber," he said. "No offense. It's just not my thang."

Natalee nodded. "I understand."

Marisol watched Percy's interaction. They were young and just having fun hanging out together—nothing too serious. But she didn't want a cute athlete, who was girl crazy and a flirt.

She knew she risked the wrath of Starr for bringing him at the last minute. But she was having so much fun that she really didn't care what Starr thought.

"Sing that Usher song," Marisol suggested, as Percy wrapped his arm around her shoulder.

"Usher?" Percy scoffed.

Natalee cleared her throat as she began to rock and snap her fingertips.

Percy looked doubtful.

"There goes my baby…boy you don't how good it feels to call you my man," she sang, closing her eyes and leaning back a little as she patted her hand against her chest.

Percy leaned back like, "Say whaaat?"

Marisol moved away from Percy and began to dance with her hand held high in the air.

Natalee sang the song like it was written for her, with all the soul and all the fire of Mary J. She hit the high notes, the riffs—all of it.

The sudden applause brought them out of their groove.

Natalee clamped her mouth shut.

Percy stopped snapping his fingers.

Marisol looked up to see Mr. Lester and his wife standing in the doorway watching them. "Hi, Mr. and Mrs. Lester," she said, pulling Percy's suit blazer closer around her bare shoulders.

Cole released his wife's hand to step forward toward Natalee. "That's a lot of voice in there," he said, picking up the hem of his tunic.

Marisol said a silent prayer that the winds didn't pick up.

"Who are you signed with?" he asked.

Natalee looked confused. "Signed?" she asked.

Sasha moved to stand beside Marisol, her eyes amused by Natalee's demeanor.

"Who's your manager?" Mr. Lester said.

Natalee shook her head. "I don't have a manager," she said.

"You should, Natalee," Sasha said. "Your voice gave me chills."

Natalee looked like she was about to faint at any moment. "My voice gave *you* chills."

Marisol laughed.

"Your father never mentioned you could sing?" Cole said, sounding slightly suspicious.

Natalee looked bashful. "He doesn't know. I usually just sing in my room."

Mr. Lester stepped back to eye her for a long time before he turned and walked away.

Marisol looked as confused as Natalee.

"That was the money shot," Sasha said softly. "Enjoy the rest of the party."

She turned and followed her husband back inside the ballroom.

Marisol leaned over and used her finger to push Percy's mouth closed. "She farts and poops just like the rest of us," she said teasingly, as she patted his chiseled jawline.

A cold wind raced across the patio, making them shiver. "Let's go in," Marisol said.

Some up-tempo song Marisol didn't know was playing, but she and Natalee headed back to their table. Percy stopped to talk to Jordan sitting on the edge of the stage alone.

Marisol followed Jordan's line of vision and saw a couple of girls—one dressed as Tinkerbell and the other a cowgirl—dancing. Starr and Dionne.

"There're the girls," Marisol said to Natalee.

They headed in their direction.

Marisol stopped suddenly and grabbed Natalee's wrist tightly. "Do not mention what just went down on the patio to Starr?"

Natalee looked a little frightened by Marisol's intensity—especially under the eerie lights—so Marisol loosened her grip and smiled.

"But I don't want to sing," Natalee protested.

"That's not the point."

Marisol noticed Starr and Dionne looking their way. She waved like she just noticed them.

"But you guys have a group?"

Starr and Dionne were headed their way.

"Starr can't sing," Marisol whispered quickly, her words running together.

"What?" Natalee asked.

"Shecantsing. Shecantsing," Marisol said urgently, just as Starr and Dionne reached them.

"There you are," Starr said.

"I've been here," Marisol said.

"Yes, you and Percy," Starr pointed out.

"Yes, *Percy and I* are having lots of fun. It's like our first non-Cooley's date," she said, turning to wave at him.

"My dad is getting on my nerves so I'm spending the night here," Dionne said, sliding into her usual spot as the peacemaker.

"Me, too," Natalee said.

"You in?" Starr asked Marisol.

Marisol nodded. What girl wouldn't want to stay up all

night filling her besties in on her BF? Plus avoid pretending to be happy about the new *bambino?*

"Definitely in," she said with a smile.

Pace Academy

The Way I See It!

GHOULY GROSS CONSUMPTION

Posted in *uncategorized* on November 1@12:02 p.m. by thedivaofdish

Horrible economy? Growing homeless population? Increase in foreclosures rates? The greatest country in the world horribly in debt?

Most people care about these things. Most. But not the Lesters. Last night was their Halloween hoedown for "charity" (side-eye! o_O). This was extravagance to the extreme according to the reports received. (Sorry no photo ops like Starr's Fashionista Fifteen Foolery.)

But here's a thought. Instead of spending two hundred fifty grand to raise probably way less than that, just cut the charity a check and scrap a party that is SO inappropriate.

The whole idea of it all scared me more than Freddy Krueger.

But not as much as what our Fakesetters will be doing in the upcoming talent show. Is being elitist a skill now?

Last but not least…this photo of the headmaster shows what he likes to do in his spare time…sneaking a booger…and in the caf of all places. Let's all say it together: Ew! Click the *link* to see the evidence and be thoroughly disgusted!

Smooches,
Pace Academy's Diva of Dish

230 comments

twenty-two

Starr

November 2@7:30 a.m. | Mood: Aggravated

Starr was livid. The Diva of Dumb had stepped on her toes one too many, many, many times since school began. But taking a below-the-belt shot at her parents with a blog post filled with lies and speculations? Humph.

"This is war," Starr said as she pulled out the cheap prepaid phone she had Marcus pick up from Well-Mart, Q-Mart, Turgett or wherever people bought them from. He had already loaded the phone with the minutes from a ten-dollar card.

As her driver, Marcus, turned her customized Range Rover through the ornate wrought-iron gates of Pace Academy, Starr barely noticed the Jaguars, Benzes, BMWs and other high-end vehicles dropping students off in front of the main building before circling out of the driveway. Marcus steered the car to the parking area reserved for visitors and parked. He knew the routine: once Marisol and Dionne arrived, then Starr would get out. The Pacesetters always walked into school together.

It was a red carpet arrival every day, especially since

the school had gotten rid of those awful uniforms. As she awaited her friends, Starr got busy trying to smoke out the blogger. She sent a link to the blog from a throwaway cell phone and then used that number to email the link to the headmaster and his loyal secretary, Mrs. Lyon.

She wanted the blogger exposed, but she didn't want to be known as a snitch.

Starr started to toss the phone, but changed her mind. *Might come in handy,* she thought, powering the phone off and shoving it deeply into her messenger bag.

Rule #1 for doing something you have absolutely no bizness doing is to tell no one. Not even your besties. It was okay to keep some secrets from friends. Right?

Starr was checking her hair and lip gloss status in her rhinestone-covered compact when she saw both Dionne's and Marisol's cars pulling into the visitors' parking lot. Marcus saw them arrive as well, and climbed out of the car to walk around and hold the door for Starr. She was careful not to scuff her new boots as she climbed out and swung her Vuitton messenger bag over her shoulder.

She wore just a pair of jeans, booties and a long-sleeved, black silk tee under a leather-trimmed wool trench coat. She was so pissed at the blogger that she didn't have the time or energy for anything more creative.

"Morning, ladies," Starr said as soon they flanked either side of her.

"That's messed up what that stupid blogger said about the party," Marisol chimed in.

"Seriously messed up," Dionne added.

Starr hitched her head higher and shrugged. "I don't

care. Let them say what they want. She's just mad because she didn't get any photos. Let her get the red carpet photos like all the other bloggers."

Marisol and Dionne laughed, moving on to other topics than the Diva of Dumb, just the way Starr wanted.

Beep.

"There is a mandatory assembly for all Pace Academy students. Instructors, please quietly escort your class to the auditorium immediately," came the announcement over the public address system.

"Th-th-that doesn't s-s-s-sound good," Ms. Pickles said, closing her textbook and looking up at the class over the rim of her wire-framed glasses. "Okay, class, pack up your belongings quietly and form a line."

"What do you think it's about, Starr?" Madelyn Jeffries said as she leaned over to whisper.

Starr shrugged at her classmate. "No clue," she said. *Don't tell me my email kicked things off already?*

As they made their way to the auditorium the halls were filled with the constant chatter of student conversations and the echo of footsteps as they made their way down the hall. Starr looked around and waved to Dionne and Marisol, who were seated with their classes. Starr settled in her seat on the end directly behind Ms. Pickles.

"Settle down, students. Settle down," Headmaster Payne said from a lectern at the center of the stage.

Starr kept her eyes on the headmaster as he pulled a handkerchief from his pocket and dabbed his upper lips and his bald head. *That is the sweatiest man,* Starr thought, frowning at the thought of what the armpits of his shirts must have looked like in his beloved houndstooth blazer.

"Now it has come to my attention that one of our students here at Pace has started a blog—"

Starr perked up, her eyes skimming the massive crowd for any sudden movements.

"I am terribly disappointed in the nature of this blog, including any posting about me," he said, self-consciously swiping at his long birdlike nose with a handkerchief.

Giggles raced across the auditorium.

"The blog is to be taken down immediately and there will be no further postings," the headmaster said, his handkerchief busy swabbing. "I am launching a full investigation into the matter and any parties affiliated with the site will be punished."

A murmur arose among the students in the auditorium. Starr glanced around, looking for a nervous face. She was far from done with the Diva or Divo of Dumb—far from it.

Starr entered the caf and paused when she saw their table filled with so much testosterone. *Is dining with boyfriends the new black for Pacesetters?*

She eyed Marisol and Percy with their heads buried over her phone. Eric was talking to Dionne and she definitely wasn't in the mood by the look on her face. And Jordan? He definitely had a tag on his toe screaming *fifth wheel.*

Taking a breath to get her ish together, Starr pulled out her chair. "Hello, people," she said, accepting the plate of fresh fruit she had already texted the girls to get for her.

"Okay, y'all, this is what it says," Marisol said, looking real cute with her side ponytail and big hoop earrings.

"What what says?" Starr asked, piercing a strawberry with her fork.

"Looks like the Diva of Dumb is done-dada," Dionne said excitedly, before glancing at Eric sideways as he tried to whisper in her ear.

Starr played it cool. Between the news of the blog and the scent of Jordan's Gucci cologne reaching her, she was an emotional wreck on the inside.

"Stop being cute and just pick the fruit up with your hand," Jordan teased, reaching across to pluck the fruit from her fork.

Starr cut her eyes up to his. They held.

"I like you, Starr," his eyes said.

"I like you, too," hers answered.

"Be mine."

"I can't."

"Why not?"

She shook her head and shifted her eyes away.

"'Looks like someone at Pace has a mouth as big as their parents' bank account. Last post. Not worth it all to help keep you losers informed,'" Marisol read.

"No more Diva of Dish," Percy said, standing up.

Starr and the whole table laughed. Soon the kids at the nearby tables joined. "No more Diva of Dish," they chanted.

Soon it spread across the whole cafeteria.

Wow, Starr thought. *Is this a sign of how much fear we all lived in worried about winding up on a dumb blog?*

Bzzz.

Starr set down her fork and picked up her iPhone. A text from Olivia with the name and email address for TopStarr's IT guru, Ethan Ndiaye.

She immediately shot him an email:

TO: Ethan.Ndiaye@TopStarr.com
FROM: Starrs_World@Yahoo.com
RE: Picking your brain
IMPORTANCE: Crucial!!!

Hi Ethan,

Could you find out the location and/or contact info for the owner of this blog site: www.paceacademyinsider.com?

It's VERY crucial.

Thanks.
Starr

Her beef with the Diva of Dumb was far from over. It was personal. Starr hit Send, satisfied that she would eventually win.

twenty-three

Dionne
November 3@7:45 p.m. | Mood: Guilty

DIONNE climbed out of her mom's Honda and jogged up the steps to her great-grandmother's house in Irvington. As always, she looked forward to their visits to her great-grandmother's house at least once a week—but most times more.

There was usually some decent home cooking (Mama Belle admitted that she didn't catch her men because of her skills at the stove), some laughter (she could out-curse Lil Duval while talking mad ish), and a little Jesus (she'd outpreach T.D. Jakes). Grandkids either got a hug or a slap, depending on their behavior—go to the left and she'd knock you back right.

The only problem with Mama Belle's house when it got cold was the temperature. She'd keep the thermostat on eighty degrees all day, every day. Dionne felt like she'd walked into an oven as soon as she opened the door. She quickly took off her coat as soon as she crossed the room to hug Ma Belle, who was sitting in her favorite recliner.

Dionne kissed her cheek, enjoying the smell of Noxzema

face cream and Avon's Timeless. "What did you cook?" Dionne asked.

Mama Belle cut her eyes at her great-granddaughter. "A big ole pot of truth," she said, her eyes locked on Dionne. "Pull up to my table."

Dionne looked over her shoulder. Her mom was nowhere to be seen. It became clear it was a setup. She slumped down onto the sofa, which was particularly scratchy because of the heat.

"When my brother and sister and I were growing up, we were so poor we had to share clothes and shoes, sleep in the same bed and pray for seconds at dinner," Mama Bell said, shifting forward in her seat to point her finger at Dionne. "And I was never ashamed of who I am and where I came from. Never!"

Dionne shifted her eyes to hide her guilt.

"We all raised you better than that foolishness, Dionne!"

She looked up, surprised by her great-grandmother's anger. "But, Mama Belle—"

Her great-grandmother's hands slashed the air, so Dionne decided to swallow the rest of her words. "You should be able to look them friends of yours in the face and say 'look where I came from and watch where I'm going.'"

"My friends know I came from Newark," she said.

Mama Belle sat up straight. "*Came from Newark?* Baby, don't you *still* live on 16th Avenue in Newark?" she asked.

"Yes, ma'am."

"If your friends can't accept you for you, and respect your mama for her, then they ain't friends worth having."

She was right, of course, and Dionne knew that as she nodded her head in agreement. But knowing what was right and doing what was right was two different things.

"Now go fix me a glass of ice water," she said.

End of conversation.

Dionne stood up and made her way across the small living room.

"And this foolishness about you sleeping in the master bedroom at your new house, cancel that," she called out. "Your mama is a good woman tryna do right by you, don't take advantage, Miss Thang."

Dang it. Dionne kissed all her plans for the master suite goodbye. When Mama Belle spoke, she listened. Period.

"When I was growing up in Newark, it was more wild and grittier than this," Risha said suddenly as she drove the streets of Newark toward home. "I remember getting off the bus in the morning and seeing blood on the corner from somebody getting shot the night before or waking up in the morning to see the street filled with police cars 'cause a woman got stabbed to death. It was crazy, you know?"

Dionne said nothing and just listened. Her parents taught her a long time ago that if you kept your mouth shut and your ears open, you'd learn a lot more.

"But I love this city. It made me into a hardworking woman," she said.

"And a good mom," Dionne added softly.

Risha nodded her head. "Yes, because I am a good mother

and I'm proud of that, because I wasn't just another teenage mother looking to get on welfare. And I raised you without public assistance."

Dionne looked out the passenger window at all the rows of new town houses and apartment buildings around their neighborhood. There was a lot of new construction and change coming to the city—her city, her hometown.

"And one day—even after we move—you will realize that this city is helping to shape who you are," she said, reaching over to lightly tap her finger against Dionne's chest.

She turned her head to lock eyes with her mother.

"I never wanted to move out of Newark, maybe into better areas of Newark. But I never thought about leaving this city. See, I gotta lot of love for this city and a lot of faith in this city..."

We're not moving. We're not moving.

"But I have a lot more faith in you," she finished.

Dionne began to smile but tried to keep it from spreading like a rainbow.

"I have narrowed it down to the house in South Orange and the one in Montclair," she said, her eyes twinkling. "Go on ahead and do the happy dance."

Dionne giggled as she snapped her fingers.

"We'll go back and look at both some time this week."

Dionne felt like she could skyrocket over the moon. "I thought about it, Mom, and I really don't want the big bedroom in either house," she said, reaching over to touch her mother's arm.

"Dionne—"

"No, listen, you have done so much for me and made so many sacrifices for me. I remember you went without so that I could have what I needed and sometimes stuff that I just wanted. I remember in the old days you giving me my food first to make sure I was full before you even ate."

Risha pulled up to a red light by Westside Park. "That's my job as a mother," she insisted, reaching up to adjust her earrings.

Dionne shook her head, swinging her ponytail back and forth. "No, some of that was overtime," she said. "So let me do something nice for you. Let me give you the big bedroom. Can I do that for you?"

Risha reached over and playfully pinched Dionne's chin. "You are a pretty good kid."

"The apple doesn't fall too far from the tree," she said, using some of Mama Belle's words of wisdom.

"Just until you are eighteen," Risha said. "If you agree, then I accept your offer."

Dionne smiled, holding out her hand with her oversize opal cocktail ring flashing. "Deal."

Risha swatted her hand away before she drove away. "You are so bourgie," she teased.

"Truly, darling, am I?" Dionne said, with a snooty accent. Risha gave Dionne her five fingers and the palm.

"South Orange or Montclair, huh?"

Dionne nodded, playing with the neon Silly Bandz she wore on her wrist. "Yeah," she answered before looking up at him sitting on the step above where she sat. They faced each other.

Their voices echoed in the hallway of the building so they talked low.

"It won't be the same with you not living in the neighborhood," Hassan said, his cute-looking face with a sad expression after hearing her news.

Dionne reached up and touched his leg through the denim fabric. "You can come and visit me and I'll come see you."

Hassan stood up on the step and then extended his hand to her. She grabbed it and let him pull her to her feet. She pursed her lips and pouted as he pulled her close to him. "I'm sorry," she said, wrapping her arms around his thin waist.

Dionne frowned at the smell of his practice jersey. "Oh God, you stink," she said, leaning back to pinch her nose.

"I stink?" he balked, pretending to smell his armpits.

Dionne stepped down, laughing and waving her hand in front of her face.

Hassan grabbed the hem of his shirt, lifted it and pulled it down over Dionne's head, shoulders and arms.

Dionne reached up to tickle his sides, desperately wanting to be free of the funky smell after hours of football practice. She stuck her head through the V-neck opening, pretending to gasp for air.

"I'm gonna miss you, Dionne," Hassan said seriously, their mouths just inches apart.

Awwww.

With a mix of sadness and excitement about the move, Dionne stood on her tiptoes and kissed her boyfriend.

"Co-sign," she said softly.

twenty-four

Marisol

November 5@4:20 p.m. | Mood: So over it!!!

"Get it, get it, get it, girrrrrl."

Marisol brought fierceness to the last eight steps of the routine as she watched herself in the mirror. Eli's coaching made her work even harder.

He came across the hardwood floors and scooped her up over his shoulder. "I think I love you," he screeched, reaching up to soundly slap her bottom.

WHAP!

Marisol laughed.

"I have a dance crush on you," he said, setting her on her feet.

Marisol felt exhilarated as she always did when she danced.

"As a matter of fact," he said, tapping his lips with his clear-coated fingernail, "I'm working on this video for a new teen group and with your look and your dancing ability you might work for the lead."

Marisol jumped up and did a high kick before she hugged

Eli close around the neck. "Oh, thanks, Eli," she said, completely gushing.

"Thanks for what?"

Marisol moved back from Eli and looked over her shoulder at Starr and Dionne finally strolling into practice. "Eli said he wanted me as a dancer in a video he's doing," Marisol said excitedly, her hands clasped together beneath her chin.

"I said *might,*" Eli stressed.

Dionne came over and hugged Marisol close. "I hope you get it, Mari," she said.

Marisol looked over Dionne's shoulder at Starr. She watched her friend arch her eyebrow. Marisol felt annoyed—big-time.

"So you want to be a video dancer?" Starr said sarcastically.

The whole happy vibe changed in an instant.

Marisol made a face. "And the problem is?" she said, her voice low but the level of her annoyance steadily rising.

"So if you're busy being a rump shaker and dropping it low, then what about the Go Gettas?" she asked.

"Starr—" Dionne said.

Marisol eyed Starr, pushing aside the urge to count to ten. "So I can't have my own dreams, Starr?" she asked.

"Oh Lawd," Eli sighed dramatically.

"Come on, y'all," Dionne said. "Let's just practice."

Starr walked up to Marisol. "Your dedication to be in our group..."

"Our group? This is all about you," Marisol snapped.

"And being a video ho ain't all about you?"

Dionne groaned and covered her face with her hands.

Eli's perfectly drawn-on eyebrows shot up.

"Better a video ho than a tone-deaf wannabe Keyshia Cole who is really a Keyshia Can't!"

Dionne and Eli gasped in shock.

"Tone-deaf?" Starr said, with attitude.

"Do-re-mi can't take your singing anymore," Marisol snapped.

Dionne stepped in between them, having to use her hands to push them both back.

"Get out, Buffy the Body!" Starr snapped, pointing her finger to the door.

"You ain't said nothin'." Marisol snatched her bag, along with Eli's business card sitting on top of it. She was leaving early for Percy's game so she had all of her things with her. She flung her scarf dramatically around her neck and strutted away. She paused when she reached the door and looked back. "And in case you're as dumb as you are tone-deaf, as far as I'm concerned the Go Gettas can go get lost."

SLAM.

Marisol actually stopped in one of the Lesters' bathrooms, showered and changed into a bedazzled jersey, leggings and Louis Vuitton sneakers. By the time she slid into the back of the Jaguar, she was so ready to see her boo Percy play.

She didn't worry about Starr or the Go Gettas. Dancing was her thing and it had nothing to do with being famous. If she was able to make it big as a dancer, then that was just icing on the cupcake. What Starr and everyone else failed to realize was that she loved to dance—even if it meant being a backup, out of the spotlight. She was fine with that—more than fine with that.

Marisol played with her diamond hoops as the Jag sped along the short distance to Pace Academy. She flipped open the armrest cover in the door, revealing a media controller and docking station. She ignored the TV set and slid her iPod into the charger. Soon the sounds of Demi Lovato filled the car.

She texted Percy:

Where u @?

"There goes my baby."

@ the football field.

She sang softly along with the music as she texted him back:

Okay. C u @ the game.

Sighing, she settled back against the leather. She looked down at her phone as her ringtone sounded. Dionne.

"Hello."

"Marisol. Oh my God, where are you?" she asked, whispering.

"On my way to the football game." Marisol slid her shades down on her nose to block some of the fall sunlight beaming through the window.

"I cannot be-lieeeeve you told Starr she can't sing," Dionne said.

Marisol had to press the phone close to her ear. "Why are you whispering?"

"We're in the studio and Starr's recording the lead vocals."

"What?!" Marisol threw her hands up.

"Yup."

"And so she still doesn't get it that she can't sing?" she asked, aware that her driver's broad shoulders were shaking with laughter.

"*O-M-G,* no. She thinks you said it to be mean."

Marisol dropped her head. "Listen, you have to tell her. You have to. This foolishness has gone on long enough—seriously."

"I can't."

"Well, sorry, but it's your problem now. I'm outta the group, thank God. As a matter of fact, I'm going to enter and do a dance routine."

Dionne sighed. "Marisol, please don't. We're friends. We can't let this group mess that up."

Marisol shook her head as if Dionne could see her. "She owes me an apology. I didn't say ish when she fired me as the choreographer. I didn't say ish when she wrote all the words like she was a solo act. I didn't even say anything when she picked out everything without even asking us, but to call me a video ho. Bump, Starr."

"Marisol—"

"I gotta go, Di. I'll holla." She ended the call.

Marisol had been friends with Starr for years and they

had had fights before. But Starr was really pushing the limit, and Marisol refused to just lie down and let Starr run all over her.

twenty-five

Starr

November 7@8:00 p.m. | *Mood: Confused*

TWO days had gone by since Starr had spoken to Marisol, and vice versa. Even though they still met in the visitors' parking lot in the morning, still ate lunch together and still met up at the lockers after school before they went their separate ways, Starr and Marisol pretended the other was invisible. It was far from their first tiff, and it wouldn't be their last.

Starr believed that Marisol would even show up to their final Go Gettas practice before the talent show. Video dancer or not, Marisol knew that when Starr set her mind to something, she was 'bout her bizness. The Go Gettas were going to be huge…and Marisol didn't want to miss out on that.

Humph, she ain't crazy, Starr thought, *is she?*

Sighing, Starr reached in her crocodile satchel for her iPhone as she climbed out of the back of her chauffeur-driven Bentley, one of two cars at her disposal.

"An email," she said, pausing outside the door of the Huntington Inn on Mills Road in Bernardsville.

FROM: Ethan.Ndiaye@TopStarr.com
TO: Starrs_World@Yahoo.com
RE: Re: Picking your brain

The domain registration for the site is private, so the info provided makes sure the true identity of the owner is protected. Trying some other things. Will get back with you soon.

Starr nodded as she slid the phone back inside her satchel. *Coming for you, Diva of Dumb,* she thought as she pulled the door open and walked inside the restaurant.

Her eyes panned the restaurant as she looked over the hostess's shoulder. Jordan looked up, spotted her and stood up with his pretty-boy swagger in his dark brown blazer, brown silk shirt and dark rinse denims. His diamond stud and chain glistened under the subtle lighting of the restaurant. He was definitely trying to get his grown man look on.

"Jordan Jackson, please," she said, smoothing her hands over her hips in her sweater dress.

Her eyes were on him as she was led to his table. He stood up when she reached the table and came around to pull out her chair to be seated.

"I'm surprised you came," he said.

"Why? We're two friends getting something to eat," she said, even as her heart beat like crazy.

"Man, come on, Starr. It's more than that," he said, reaching across the table to touch her hand.

"Jordan," she began.

"Starr, you have to give me a chance and stop thinking the worst about being my girl," he said, folding his arms on the table and leaning in to look at her.

"Straight up, Jordan, I'm not having sex."

Jordan threw his hands up, drawing the curious stares of several diners. "I didn't ask you to."

"In time you would have," she said, sitting back to cross her slender arms over her chest as she crossed her legs.

"Why do you think that?" he asked.

"Once you taste the goodies, there's no going back."

Jordan took a sip of his ice water, looking at her over the rim of the glass. "Are you trying to ask me if I've had sex?"

Starr snorted. "Are you trying to convince me you haven't?" she countered.

"I'm trying to figure out why you're acting like you don't like me like that."

Starr sighed as she picked up the leather-bound menu. "I do like you, Jordan," she admitted, using the menu to hide the warmth filling her cheeks.

He reached over to lower the menu. "I like you, too, Starr," he said.

She looked away to avoid the truth of his words in his eyes. “I want sushi,” she said.

Jordan nodded his head and picked up his own menu. “Nah, I don’t do sushi. I want a steak,” he said, looking down at the menu.

Starr allowed her eyes to roam over his face. When Jordan had texted her that he wanted to go eat and talk, Starr was not going to show. Her daddy had talked to her about little boys and the things they want from little girls—if they let them.

Starr wasn’t letting anybody do anything. Her mother taught her about the importance of a girl maintaining her reputation. She remembered the conversation well. “Once a woman gets a reputation for being a ho, you can never change it. That is how people always view her, regardless of whether she’s no longer promiscuous. It’s not fair in life, but lots of things aren’t fair. Always remember that as a woman your reputation is everything,” her mother had said.

The pitfalls of having sex had been clearly imparted by her parents. She couldn’t—and wouldn’t—forget it. Jordan was moving in a faster, more experienced lane than she was and although Starr liked him she didn’t want to tempt fate.

“Are we cool?” Jordan asked.

Starr nodded, quickly shifting her eyes from his face. “We’re cool, but we’re just friends,” she stressed.

“If that’s all you have for me then I’ll take it,” he said with a big smile.

"Trust and believe that's all I have for you," Starr reassured him with a serious expression.

Jordan reached across the table and captured her hand again. "But I'm not giving up on us," he promised, tilting his head to the side to charm her with his eyes.

Starr couldn't break their gaze and she couldn't stop her heart from being happy that he wasn't going to give up.

As soon as Starr walked into the house, she kicked off her shoes. Picking them up in her hand, she padded barefoot to the elevator and rode down to the basement. Both her parents' cars were in the garage, and she knew they were in the studio.

Sure enough, she found them there. Her mom was in the recording booth and Dad was controlling the digital equipment. She stood in the doorway and watched them. Her father's eyes were locked on her mom as Sasha held the earphones and closed her eyes and sang.

She entered the room and took the stool next to her father. "She looks so happy," Starr said softly.

"Your mother lives for her music," Cole said, adjusting sound levels.

"But won't it take her away from home?" Starr asked.

Cole turned and leaned back in the chair, eyeing her through his ever-present shades. "You think your mama's going to put her career before her children?" he asked.

Yes. "Daddy, I'm old enough to remember Mama being on tour for most of the year," she reminded him.

"Why do you think your mama is a singer?" he asked, still watching her as the sounds of her mother singing a ballad filled the air.

"For fame," she said.

Cole shook his head.

"No, she does it because she loves to write and produce music, she feels alive performing onstage, and she loves to hear from fans about them connecting with something emotional in her music," he explained. "The fame, bright lights and money come after that, not because of it."

Starr shifted her eyes to her mother. "So you should do what you love first," she said.

Sasha ended the song and removed her headphones to walk out of the booth. She walked over and hugged Starr to her side. "How's my baby girl?"

"Sad because you'll be touring a lot," Starr said, hugging her back.

"Awww," Sasha said playfully.

"Okay, Sasha, let's listen to the playback," Cole said, reaching for the console button, his huge diamond ring blindingly bright as it caught the light.

"Take it from the top?" Sasha asked.

Cole looked over at her, his hand shifting a bit as he nodded and hit the buttons.

Starr's eyes widened as Fiyah's track for the slow jam filled the air. She stepped forward to hit the playback music. "That's not—"

Cole knocked her hand away. "I like the track," he said.

Suddenly Starr's voice filled the air. She was nervous. She didn't want her parents to find out about her musical aspirations like that.

Cole and Sasha frowned deeply.

Starr buried her face in her hands.

"Who in the tone-deaf hell is that?" he asked.

Starr gasped as she looked at him aghast. "Daddy," she whined, swatting his shoulder.

He looked over his shoulder at her before he turned the track off. "What?" he asked, seemingly lost.

"You don't like my singing, Daddy?" Starr asked.

Cole slumped back in his chair and lifted his shades to look at his daughter. "Huh?" he asked.

Sasha grabbed Starr's shoulders and turned her toward her. "What's going on?" she asked.

Starr felt like her stomach was on fire. She was hurt and embarrassed to have her father co-sign Marisol's take on her singing. *I can't sing.*

She explained her plans for the Go Gettas group—all of it, the team, the talent show, the demo, everything.

"Well, you've been mighty busy, Starr," her mother said, crossing her arms over her chest as she leaned over to eye her husband. (Translation: Say or do something.)

Cole released a heavy sigh as he leaned forward and patted the empty leather stool next to him. "Come on, baby girl, let's talk."

"About what, Daddy?" she asked in her best princess voice, which usually got her whatever she wanted.

"About your skills, which are better suited to management than performing," he began lightly.

twenty-six

Dionne
November 7@8:15 p.m. | Mood: Pampered

"All done."

Dionne was spun around in the chair by the makeup artist. She clapped, turning this way and that, as she studied her face. For the first shots of the hip-hop kids' magazine layout, her makeup had been light, airy and fresh to go with the candy-store backdrop in the photos. Now her makeup was just a little edgier to match the Mohawk they had shaped her hair and the black leather outfit she wore. She called it tougher than leather, but prettier than ever.

"I love it," she sighed with a big toothy grin.

She turned in her chair, looking past the photographer, stylist and makeup people milling around the studio to look for her dad and Hassan.

Dionne was superexcited that her mom and dad had given her permission to invite Hassan to attend the shoot. She hated excluding him from this part of her life and saw the photo shoot as a chance to let him know that she wanted him in her world or at least a part of it.

She smiled seeing him talk to her parents. *Hassan looks*

so cute, she thought, *in his long-sleeved V-neck shirt and cargo khakis that match his Timberlands. Swag on ten.*

Awwww, I heart him, she thought, feeling her heart swell with first-love emotions.

He wasn't nervous around her dad since Hassan knew her father from before he was the Don. And they knew him. He'd been her friend since their days at South 17th Street Elementary School.

The photography assistant motioned for Dionne and her father. She gave Hassan a smile and he raised his phone to snap a shot of her as they positioned her beside her dad in front of a white backdrop.

As soon as the flash went off, Dionne locked in on the lens, remembering everything she'd learned from Tyra Banks on *America's Next Top Model.*

All about the eyes.

"Good. Good," said the photographer, a tall, skinny guy, who looked like an animated bobblehead doll.

Dionne didn't turn it off until the photographer yelled, "That's a wrap."

"Had fun?" Lahron asked, sliding his shades up onto his face as an assistant helped Dionne into a robe and handed her a bottle of water.

"Yes, Daddy. It was so much fun," she said, her heart still racing.

Truly, she hated for it to end…especially since Candylixxxious was nowhere in sight. Some other rapper needed her services down in Miami for a video shoot. *Bye bye, boo, be gone.*

Dionne made her way to the dressing room to change

back into her clothes. "I'm keeping the hair and makeup," she said, loving the slightly edgier look.

As soon as she was done, she made her way back to her father and Hassan. "Let's roll," she told them, two-stepping and snapping her fingers.

Mindy, her dad's personal assistant, handed him one of his phones. As they left the building, Dionne and Hassan walked ahead.

"Thanks for asking if I could come," Hassan said.

"Can you believe all the rappers we saw?" she said.

"I hated to be a fan, but I got a few autographs," he said with a shrug.

"That's cool."

Hassan shoved his hands deep into the pockets of his pants. "You ever felt like you went from watching rich kids on TV to being one?"

"Sometimes the change is a lot to swallow, but mostly it's fun," she told him truthfully.

"Since you're moving, you think any part of Newark is gonna fit into your life anymore?"

Dionne looked up at him, and felt like the question really was, "Will I fit into your life anymore?"

"I'm not turning my back on my hometown or my homeboy," she said, trying to lighten the mood.

"Your homeboy," Hassan balked, glancing at her.

She playfully punched his shoulder as she circled him with a homeboy stroll. "Yo, yo, you, whaddit do, son?" she asked, with a heavy New York accent.

Hassan laughed, smiling as they reached the outside. Her

father's Denali awaited them and they all climbed in, while her father continued talking on his phone.

"I don't know what I would do if my dad went from being a garbage man to a rich and famous anything," Hassan said.

Bzzz.

Dionne pulled out her BlackBerry.

Where are you?

"Who's that, your other homeboy?" Hassan asked, lightly tapping her thigh with his fist.

"No, my home girl," she said, her deep purple nails flying away.

On the way from photo shoot.

"You still in the middle of your two friends?" he asked.

"Yes, and it's crazy. In Newark when you're mad at somebody you're mad, and you give each other fifty feet or better," Dionne said, tapping her BlackBerry against her leg as she awaited Starr's response. "But these two chicks just ignore each other. I'm sitting there having two different conversations sometimes."

Hassan laughed.

"And then on top of it, Marisol quit the Go Gettas. Starr can't sing, and I still haven't finished my rap," she said.

Hassan frowned. "Do you really want to be in the group?" he asked, making a face.

Dionne sat back. "I did at first, before all the drama. But now..."

With all of her free time spent with Hassan, and even though she knew she had to go another round with the sixteen bars, her motivation was gone. Without Marisol, the Go Gettas were just weird and awkward.

"To be honest, the thought of performing at the talent shows makes me feel sick," she admitted.

"Then drop out until y'all get everything straight."

Her dad turned around in his seat and eyed her through his shades. "A part of being a good friend is telling them when they're wrong and when they're right. You have to tackle the good times and the bad," he said.

"Tell Starr she can't sing?" she asked.

"Better you tell her than everybody at the talent show throwing tomatoes," her father said.

"That would be mad crazy," Hassan added.

"A real friend wouldn't let her get embarrassed like that."

"But Marisol told her and she didn't believe it," Dionne insisted.

"Wow," Hassan said, covering his mouth and trying not to laugh.

Dionne shook her head.

"Honesty is the best policy, ya hear me?" Dionne's father said, shaking his wrist to ease his diamond watch down to his wrist.

Her life reminded her of the end of every episode of *Sesame Street.* The word for today was *honesty.*

She thought about all the lies she'd told and even more lies that she told to cover herself. The hole was getting deeper and deeper and she felt like it was going to be harder and harder to get out.

twenty-seven

Marisol

November 8@8:20 p.m. | Mood: Shocked

Marisol was lying on the bed in her bare feet, with her feet high in the air as she talked to Percy.

"Man, you farted?" someone hollered in the background.

Marisol frowned. "Is that your brother?" she asked, her face a mask of distaste.

Percy laughed. "Man, that's life," he said to whomever he offended in the background.

Beep.

Marisol's frown deepened. "Hold on. I got another call."

Click.

"Hi, Marisol."

"Who's this?" she asked, pulling her phone from her face to look at the incoming number.

"Natalee. You busy?"

"Kinda sorta on the phone with the BF," she said, remembering that they all exchanged numbers at the sleepover Halloween night.

"Well, I hate to bother you, but you said not to tell Starr that her dad liked my singing, and Dionne is at a photo shoot with her dad," she said.

"Whassup?"

"Mr. Lester called my dad about me doing a three-song demo for his record company."

Marisol squealed excitedly and kicked her feet in the air. "That's what's up, Natalee," she said, truly happy for the chica.

"My dad wants me to do it…but I'm not sure."

Beep.

"Hold on, Natalee."

Click.

"Why'd you hang up?" Percy asked. "You act like you could smell the fart through the phone."

Marisol rolled her eyes. Boys! "Hold on, okay?"

Click.

"Natalee, listen. I'm going to pick you up tomorrow and we'll go to the talent show together and talk about this record deal you're so scared of."

"Text me the deets," she said before hanging up.

Click.

Marisol held the phone away as Percy let out a huge belch that reminded her of the drunken dude on *The Simpsons.*

"Oh my God, that was so lame," she said.

"I didn't know you were back."

"Still."

"We had chili for dinner," he said, as an explanation.

"Per—"

"Marisol," her father said as he walked in the room carrying a black garment bag.

She quickly ended the call, deleted the last entry and powered down before he reached her bed.

"Your mother is not feeling well so she can't attend this event with me. Want to go?" he asked.

Marisol popped up and rolled off the bed to take the outstretched garment bag. She unzipped it quickly but carefully, shrieking in surprise at the raspberry strapless dress with tiers of ruffles from mid-hip down to just below her knee. She checked the label—a creature of habit. Caroline Herrera. Loving it.

"Give me thirty minutes," she said, turning to run into her walk-in closet for accessories.

"No, I lost time going to buy the dress. I can give you ten minutes," he said in his tuxedo, looking down at his watch.

Marisol headed towards her bath and turned back to her father. "Fifteen, Papi," she called over her shoulder, dashing to the bathroom.

Eighteen minutes later, she walked out of the bathroom and posed. "Let me grab my shoes and a purse and we can go," she said.

"That's my girl," her dad said, rising to his feet.

On her way to the closet, she eyed her cell phone on the bed and wondered if her father had powered it on and gone through it.

Marisol slipped on a pair of pale gold stacked heels and covered the dress with a short fitted satin blazer and grabbed a deep purple bag. She smiled as she stepped out of the closet and her father bent his arm and bowed slightly.

Marisol felt like a princess being escorted to the ball.

Marisol yawned deeply, eliciting a nudge from her father under their table. "Sorry," she said, sounding sleepy.

She was bored to tears.

"I'm going to find the bathroom," she said, as she picked up her egg-shaped purse from the table. As soon as she was out of her father's sight, she powered on her phone and called her voice mail.

Beep.

"Marisol, this is Starr. We need to talk. Call me."

She arched an eyebrow as she saved the message—just in case she needed proof that Starr had called her first. Yes! Marisol punched the air.

"I'll call her later," she said as she texted Percy.

With Dad. Call u later.

Marisol hit Send and waited in the elaborate hall outside the venue where the dinner was being held.

"There goes my baby..."

Marisol rushed to open the text.

Tell ur dad ILY 4 me. LMBO.

She rolled her eyes. She wished she could tell her dad that some boy said he loves you.

"There goes my baby..."

Have fun. TTYL.

Marisol looked up just as Kimora emerged from the ballroom in a beautiful, red strapless dress. The theme song to her reality show—which the Pacesetters used to watch together faithfully—played in her head.

"It's the fabulous, fabulous..."

She watched as Kimora headed toward the bathroom, her long black hair flowing in soft curls down her back, with the tips of her heels barely peeking out from the dress.

"It's the fabulous, fabulous..."

Marisol paused for just a second before she took off behind her.

Marisol was lying across her bed in the darkness, enjoying the sound of silence and trying to get her thoughts together. Sleep was her enemy.

She started to get up and throw on some dance gear to try to tire herself out by dancing, but decided against it.

She glanced at the clock. It was just after midnight. Percy had already fallen asleep on the phone. Dionne's mom would trip if she called that late at night.

Starr.

No. Marisol wasn't ready yet.

She left the bed and her room. The entire house was quiet and dimly lit. It didn't matter. She could find her way in total darkness, having roamed the house since she was younger than Carlos.

Marisol was surprised to find her father sitting in the kitchen with a big bowl of ice cream in front of him. "That looks good," she said, standing on the other side of the island.

Alex stood up and retrieved a spoon from the drawer—a silent invitation to share. Marisol came around the table and took the spoon.

It had been a while since they had shared any father-daughter moments. And the mess of his recent affair had created a wide gap between them that she was just beginning to come to terms with. She had missed her father.

"Only a man—or little girl—with troubles can't sleep at this hour," he said.

Marisol dipped her spoon into the bowl, coming up with a big glob of ice cream and miniature Reese's cup. "Starr and I fell out," she said.

"Because?"

"She came up with the idea for a girl group and then she insulted my routines, fired me as the choreographer, and then when the choreographer she hired told me I dance so well that maybe he can get me in a video..."

Alex frowned deeply.

"For a new teen group, Papi," she clarified. "And he hasn't said anything else or I would have talked to you and Mami."

His shoulders relaxed just a bit. "The answer is no whenever the time does come...but continue."

Me and my big mouth, she thought, reminding herself to think before she spoke. "Anyway, Starr is on this quest to be famous, and not just because of her parents, but she's being all controlling, all dictating...all Starr."

Alex smiled. "And?"

"And I quit the group."

"Because?"

"Fame shouldn't cost a friendship," she said. "It's not everything."

"Exactly."

Huh?

"Marisol, listen, fame is all about how you use it and what it means to you," her father said.

She looked at her dad.

"I've been a victim of my fame before," he admitted, pushing the rest of the bowl of ice cream toward her. "But your mother has taught me that I can find balance through this craziness by using the fame to do good deeds—to help people. To try my best to make the world a better place, not just enjoy the fruits of my labor, but to harvest the seeds and plant them and grow fruits for someone else to enjoy as well. Does that make sense?"

Marisol nodded.

"Now it's up to you to decide how to handle your friendship with Starr—that's a part of growing up. But before you do anything that major like joining a group you have to decide, is it something you really want? Is it?"

Marisol shook her head no.

"Then don't do it," he said simply, bending to kiss her forehead. "Do not stay up too late."

Papi, life is not that easy, she thought as he shuffled out of the kitchen.

Marisol stirred the melting ice cream. She forgave Starr for the foolishness, but there was no way she was getting back in the Go Gettas—even though Starr couldn't sing her way out of a Fucci (fake Gucci) bag. Marisol didn't doubt that somehow, someway, Starr was going to make the Go Gettas work. Even if it meant using digital equipment to enhance her voice. But the talent show?

She was willing to do that if—and it was a humongous *if*—there was a fix for that train wreck waiting to happen.

twenty-eight

Starr

November 10@7:20 p.m. | Mood: Big-time scared

Pace Academy was alive with the excitement of the night. The students were busy doing last-minute preparations for the talent show even as the parking lot and the auditorium began to fill up with their friends and family.

Starr had commandeered a classroom for the Go Gettas to perform, and she nervously paced in her blinged-out Louis Vuitton high-top sneakers. She hated how nervous she felt—absolutely hated it. She was sure she was going to sweat through her costume and have her makeup melting off her face like a popsicle sitting in the sun.

"Chill, Starr. If Marisol said she's coming, she's coming," Dionne said from her perch as she got her makeup done.

The room bustled with the Go Gettas team. Eli was there in a sequined tuxedo jacket and jeans ready to run through their dance routine one last time before their performance. Their stylist was packing up the outfits and accessories she had laid out on a wooden desk for them to choose from. The glam squad had their makeup cases strewn about the teacher's desk and they'd transformed the girls from cute to fabulous.

Where are you, Marisol?

When her friend had texted her around one o'clock that morning, Starr had truly been happy that Marisol had accepted her sort-of apology. Starr had called her and then they called in Dionne and they stayed on the phone for an hour working out their differences, planning how to make their talent show performance a success.

No one had wanted to back out of the talent show, since some of the kids at Pace would have *loved* to see the Pacesetters show signs of weakness.

Nothing.

Starr whipped out her iPhone and called Marisol again. "Where are you?" she asked urgently.

"Still getting things ready," she said, sounding out of breath.

Starr heard the first *boom-boom* of the music. "It's started, Marisol," she stressed, leaving the classroom to head to the closed doors of the auditorium.

"Okay, on the way right now."

Starr ended the call as she opened the door and stood in the back against the wall. Her eyes scanned the dimly lit auditorium as Hector Manuel played the piano. She saw Marisol's parents and her little brother, Carlos, in his seat making faces at some girl sitting behind him. She saw Jordan and his friends sitting near the back of the auditorium. (Because of his record deal he'd decided not to perform in the talent show. Felt he had an unfair advantage. Whatevs.) Dionne's dad and some woman she didn't recognize sat in the middle. *Is that Dionne's mom?* she wondered, realizing just then that she'd never met her mother before.

Her eyes continued to search for her parents, but she didn't see them. She was disappointed. Her parents were so busy living the life of celebrities that they sometimes forgot the normal everyday life things—like attending your kid's talent show.

It had been a hard pill to swallow for her parents to tell her that she wasn't hitting any of the right notes.

Starr just assumed that because her mother could sing, so could she.

Wrong. Her parents wouldn't lie to her. And even though Marisol said it in a hurtful way, she hadn't lied to her either. *Fine, I won't be singing my way to fame. That's cool. There's more than one way to conquer the world. Some did it with talent, but most did not.* She was a smart girl and her parents taught her early on that by being educated and well-informed, the world could be yours.

Starr shifted her eyes back to the stage as Hector took his stand and bowed as the crowd applauded politely.

Headmaster Payne made his way onto the stage, his handkerchief ready to sop up his perspiration. "Let's welcome to the Pace Academy stage Jennifer Killings, who will be doing a soliloquy from *Hamlet*."

Starr watched the light-skinned daughter of a trucking magnate take the stage in an elaborate Elizabethan costume.

She watched her and four more acts, including a dance solo from Marisol's archnemesis.

This place needs some life, she thought, trying hard not to yawn like some of the parents were doing as they shifted about in their seats.

The headmaster took to the stage again. "Next up is Gary Henderson and his amazing accordion," he stumbled.

Starr rolled her eyes as the second coming of Steve Urkel walked out onstage. That was Starr's cue to exit. She didn't do accordions.

She walked out into the auditorium, preparing to call her parents.

"Starr!" She looked up at Jordan sticking his head out the door.

"Good luck…friend," he stressed with a toothy grin.

"Thank you, friend," she said, turning to continue down the hall back to the Go Gettas headquarters.

Dionne's makeup was done. She batted her full eyelashes at Starr. "Love the lashes. Love them," she said as their stylist worked behind her to tighten the corset over her T-shirt and black ballerina skirt and leggings.

The door to the classroom opened and Marisol flew in, still breathing hard from her mad dash to get everything done.

Starr's elaborately made-up eyes widened. "Where is she?"

"Right behind me."

Starr nodded. "Good. Then let's do this!"

"And coming to the stage next is a group calling themselves the Go Gettas." The headmaster rushed off the stage as the lights dimmed and the girls rushed onto the stage in the darkness to take their spots.

Starr posed, knowing Eli stood in the wings watching them like a hawk.

"We are the Go Gettas. We are here to entertain you. Sit back. Chillax. And watch how we work," they said in unison.

The audience stirred in excitement as the music started at the exact moment the lights flickered on and off as they did robotic movements.

BOOM!

The lights came up and the girls—Starr, Dionne, Marisol and Natalee—all started their dance routine. The crowd went wild like the girls gave them life.

Dionne stepped up first, adjusting her mic slightly:

Watch this Brick City baby
Turn it up and turn loose…hey
Me and my girls yeah
You know we got that juice…hey
We're the real Go Gettas
Having fun, setting trends…wow
Making all them ends
Dominating all over y'all

"We're the Go Gettas," the girls sang. "The Go Gettas… Go Gettas. Yeah!"

Starr smiled as they danced around the stage, each one taking their turn to really get loose. She was having fun. Period. All the pressure of trying to sing her way to fame was gone. All the drama of alienating her friends—done.

Dionne spit another rhyme and Starr's thoughts were on

the next part of the show. She eyed Natalee and gave her a wink to let her know not to be scared.

It was Marisol's idea to bring her into the group. Even though Starr knew she might regret Natalee being drawn deeper and deeper into their clique (including her parents enrolling her at Pace that morning so that she could be in the talent show), she knew Natalee was going to save them from being laughed off the stage.

It was hard to swallow, but the girl could sing...especially after admitting that she couldn't. But she wouldn't forget how cool it was for her to spend all day learning the routines and the music to help the Pacesetters out.

"We're the Go Gettas, Go Gettas," Starr lip-synched, making sure nothing came out her mouth.

Right on cue they posed with their legs wide and one arm high in the air.

BOOM!

The stage light went black and the up-tempo music faded away. The crowd applauded and went wild. Starr was loving it. She didn't even care that they had scrapped her original Go Gettas song and made it mostly a rap.

From the darkness, Natalee did a soulful run that quieted the crowd down again. The lights popped back on and Starr smiled at Natalee as she flung her head back and came right in on time with the first verse:

My heart...just won't let go
My feelings for you...they must grow
My love...it's hard not to show
Because my heart won't go.

My heart…oh no, it won't let go.
I can't have you, why won't it let go?

As the Pacesetters did a simple two-step in the background, Starr had to admit the chick could sing. Forget being a good singer for a white girl, she was a good singer *period.*

Natalee gave Starr's song life and she was big-time proud of herself for writing it. Having cancelled Fiyah's trip, she felt a little disappointed that no one would ever hear the song beyond tonight.

Natalee ended the song and the four of them bowed to thunderous applause and whistles from the audience.

The Pacesetters had once again cemented their spot as the ones to beat.

Starr looked out in that moment and saw her parents on their feet applauding just as loudly as everyone else. And in that moment, everything was right with the world.

twenty-nine

Dionne
November 10@9:35 p.m. | Mood: Proud

The girls all rushed off the stage with the audience still on their feet. They hugged each other and jumped up and down excitedly.

"*O-M-G.* Y'all, we did soooo good," Marisol said.

"I can't believe we pulled it off," Starr admitted with a smile as they all tried to catch their breath.

"We shut it down," Dionne said, still feeling the excitement from their performance.

"Good job, ladies," Headmaster Payne said. "And welcome to Pace, Miss Livingston."

"Thank you," she said, her voice deep and husky after just singing her butt off.

Dionne shifted her eyes to Starr to see how she was handling it all, but she was surprised (and happy) to see that Starr just looked happy.

"Thank you all for coming to tonight's talent show," the headmaster said as he stood center stage. "First, a little school business if you all don't mind," he continued. "Due to some consistent and thoroughly inappropriate violations of the dress code, the board held an emergency meeting tonight before the talent show and voted to reinstate our uniform policy effective immediately."

Every student in the audience moaned, some even booed and hissed. The Pacesetters all eyed one another in surprise and disappointment.

Headmaster Payne cleared his throat. "And the winner of the five-hundred-dollar cash prize is…"

There was a drum roll.

"The Go Gettas."

The girls screeched, instantly forgetting the blow to their wardrobe at Pace, as they ran onstage. Marisol grabbed the envelope and the mic as the audience applauded.

"Thank you. Thank you. We just wanted everyone to know that we have decided to donate the prize money to a charity to be decided at a later time."

Huh? Who decided that? Dionne thought as she continued to smile and applaud. Natalee's and Starr's faces were just as confused as hers.

All the other talent show contestants rushed onstage to congratulate them and Dionne pushed aside the money issue. None of the girls was hurting for cash anyway.

It took them at least twenty minutes to make it off the stage and into the auditorium to find their parents. Dionne headed straight for her mother and father, glad that they survived a night sitting together without arguing.

"You did good, my little Brick City baby," Risha said, looking nice in a wrap dress and heels—so different from her usual uniforms or jeans.

Dionne had decided to pay homage to her hometown in

her rap. Once she made that choice, finally the sixteen bars easily came to her. It was her way of saying goodbye to her city since they had purchased the house in South Orange.

Lahron the Don took his fitted cap off and set it on his daughter's head. "Regular chip off the fly block," he joked, before hugging her close to his side in his linen military-style shirt and jeans.

"Thanks," she said.

She wished Hassan could have come, but he had a game. She wasn't quite ready to introduce him to her friends. Not yet. Although she missed him like crazy, everything had worked out for the best.

She searched the crowd for her friends. "I want you to meet my friends," she said, still holding her mother's hand.

Risha squeezed her hand and looked surprised. "Really? Me? I can come out of the closet now," she joked.

Dionne pushed aside her guilt. "I'll be right back," she said, moving through the crowd of people filling the halls outside the auditorium.

It took her a minute to gather up Starr and Marisol, but soon she was pulling them behind her toward her parents.

"You did pick a good school, Lahron, so congrats on doing something right," she heard her mom say.

"You really need to look into why you stay mad at me, baby," he snapped back.

"I ain't your baby," she snapped.

"You wanna be."

Dionne froze, deathly afraid her parents were about to have one of the balls-to-walls arguments. "Hey, y'all," she called out, hoping Starr and Marisol had missed the exchange.

Risha and Lahron turned their heads to look at Dionne and the girls with big grins. Thank God.

"Chitchat with Daddy about why he think Mama still likes him," she added.

"Ma, Pops, this is Starr, the bossy one," Dionne said with a grin.

"Huh?" Starr said playfully, as she looked at Dionne before she stepped forward to offer them both her hand. "Hi, Mr. Hunt. Nice to meet you, Mrs. Hunt."

Dionne saw her mother frown. "We weren't mar—"

"And this is Marisol, the sassy one," Dionne said, completely cutting her mother off.

Marisol stepped forward and hugged Risha excitedly, giving each of her cheeks a kiss. "Nice to meet you."

Dionne looked over her shoulder and saw Natalee standing by her parents, looking over at them with her usual bored expression. Oops. She headed right toward her. "Hello, Mr. and Mrs. Livingston," she said politely. "Can I steal Natalee for a second?"

"As long as you bring her back," Mr. Livingston joked.

Dionne smiled before pulling her toward her parents and the other girls. "And this is Natalee, the new one," Dionne said.

"Hi," Natalee said, waving her thin white hand.

"Little girl, you got some pipes on you," Lahron the Don said.

Natalee smiled.

Starr looked bored.

Marisol looked proud.

"So what's up with the Go Gettas now?" Risha asked.

Watch Mama now.

"This was it. We're retired," Starr stepped up to say.

"Awww. Too bad," Risha said.

Dionne and her dad cut her a knowing glance, since she was against the group from the start. "Can I stay at Starr's?" Dionne asked.

Risha shrugged. "That's fine with me just as long as the girls come and stay with you sometime," she said.

Baby steps, Mama, baby steps.

"After we move," Dionne added, giving her mother a hard look.

"Of course," Risha said.

The girls all walked back to their parents with a final wave. Dionne eyed them. "Mama, please be safe on that road home. Call me as soon as you get there."

"Who said I'm going home?" Risha responded with sass. "Mama might have plans for the weekend."

Dionne remembered the look on her mom's face that time she was on the phone.

Lahron snorted in the back of his throat.

Dionne remembered the god-awful sight of Candylixxxious's barely covered butt as she strutted around her father's apartment.

Daddy was living the life. Maybe Mama needed a little love, too.

"Are you trying to say I don't have, won't have, or can't have a man?" Risha snapped.

Dionne grabbed both their hands. "Let me walk y'all to

your cars," she said, knowing there was no way she could leave the two of them alone. It was best to send them both on their separate ways.

thirty

Marisol

November 10@10:35 p.m. | *Mood: Proud*

Marisol's eyes searched the crowd for Percy. She knew he was here, but where did he go? As the girls made their way back to the Go Gettas glam station, Marisol headed straight for her pocketbook and pulled out her cell phone to text Percy.

Where r u?

Everyone in the room was still buzzing about their performance as they finished packing up their things. Marisol felt her stomach get weak with nervous energy. Something didn't feel right.

"There goes my baby..."

Marisol almost dropped the phone as she scrambled to answer.

"Love is a dangerous game," Starr drawled.

On the way home.

She frowned. He'd left without even seeing her and saying goodbye. That was big-time weird. She didn't bother to even text him back.

"Boys are big-time dumb," she mumbled, slamming her things into her overnight bag. "I hope my mama is having a girl so that she doesn't add to the male population."

"Your mom's pregnant?" Starr asked, saying it like the idea of it was similar to a dog giving birth to a cat.

Marisol nodded.

Eli tugged at one of her shoulder-length ebony curls. "Honey, don't ever let a boy stress you out. It leads to bad skin and muffin tops over your jeans," he said.

Marisol smiled.

"Plus I got you an audition for the video, so I need you focused," he whispered to her.

Marisol perked up. "Really?" she mouthed to him, her eyes bright.

He nodded.

She was glad he didn't broadcast it because Marisol didn't know if Starr could take it. She handled Natalee being the lead and even cracked jokes about her singing—or lack thereof.

As they finally packed up and left the now-empty school, Marisol was imagining her dance performance in her head. *Maybe I should hire someone to choreograph something fierce for me,* she thought as they all climbed in Starr's Range Rover parked behind her parents' waiting Denali. She barely heard any of the girls' excited chatter. Her thoughts floated back and forth between her audition and Percy.

"Your mom is cool, Dionne," Starr said.

"Yeah, we're real close," Dionne answered.

Marisol was sitting by the door and she turned her head to lean forward to look at her. "I didn't know you were moving," she said.

"Yeah, my dad bought us a house in South Orange and we want to be in it before Thanksgiving," she said.

Marisol reached in her purse for her lip gloss. She happened to look up just as they drove past Cooley's and peeked inside the brightly lit restaurant. She gasped at the sight of Percy and some girl with an ultrashort hairdo who she didn't know sitting at a table in front of the window.

The girls' chatter continued around her as Marisol turned in her seat to keep her eyes locked on the sight of Percy laughing as the girl made motions with her hands.

Percy was a cheater?

Marisol's stomach was hot and her heart pounded like crazy as she whipped out her phone and dialed his number. He never answered. Three times it went to voice mail.

Not wanting to alert the girls to her drama she texted him:

U & ur boo look real good 2gthr in Cooley's. Do I even have 2 say u need 2 give me 50ft from now on? On to the next 1.

She hit Send without any hesitation.

Boys were all about *drama*.

"What's wrong, Marisol?" Dionne asked.

Tears were filling her eyes but Marisol shook her head. "Nothing," she said.

Starr whipped her head around from her seat in the front by the driver. "What happened, Marisol?" she asked.

"I just saw Percy at Cooley's…with another giiirrlll," she wailed before the waterworks kicked off.

"Awww," everyone sighed in unison.

"Marcus, take us back to Cooley's, please," Starr said, reaching back to squeeze one of Marisol's trembling hands.

Dionne took the other.

Natalee reached behind Dionne to pat Marisol's shoulder.

Their kindness made her cry even harder until she was trying to keep snot from running out her nose. By the time they circled the block and came back and pulled up in front of Cooley's, Percy and his mysterious date were long gone.

thirty-one

Dionne

November 26@9:00 a.m. | Mood: Thankful

DIONNE rolled over onto her back and nestled in the middle of her bed as she looked up at the octagon-shaped skylight above. The skies had never looked bluer and the leaves on the towering trees had never looked brighter. She truly had so much to be thankful for as she looked around her spacious, new bedroom. It didn't have the grandeur of her mother's suite but was a miniature replica of the larger master bedroom complete with its own fireplace, spa bathroom, walk-in closet and mini-balcony that really was just big enough for her to stand on to get some fresh air.

She rolled out of bed in her warm and toasty pajamas, making it as neat as a pin before she headed to the bathroom. Her outfit for the day was already laid out on the chaise longue in the corner of the room, but she threw on sweats and a tank top after her shower and headed down the stairs to the kitchen.

The smells of Thanksgiving were in the air. Dionne's stomach growled, but she'd already planned to skip breakfast to keep puh-lenty of room for the turkey and all the fixings.

"Mornin'," she said, eyeing her mother and Mama Belle cooking away.

They looked up at her. "Cut up the collards," Mama Belle said.

Dionne could only shake her head because she knew there was no time for niceties. There was work to do and some of it had her name written all over it.

She used the remote to turn on the small flat-screen TV over the kitchen table. They always watched the Thanksgiving Day parade. Always.

"Dionne, you talk to your daddy?" Risha asked as she opened the oven door to check on the turkey and to slide Mama Belle's six sweet potato pies in the other oven.

"Yeah."

Mama Belle cleared her throat.

"I mean yes, ma'am."

The older woman nodded approvingly.

"Your grandma Les coming?"

Dionne glanced at Risha because she knew her mother and her father's mother never really got along.

"Yes, and thank you for inviting her, Ma."

Risha shrugged, but it was major that she even extended an invite to her. For several years now they hadn't spoken, and once Lahron hit it big with his music the tension between them had just gotten worse.

Risha's mother had passed when she was just ten and Dionne never had the chance to meet her.

"They should be here around one, Ma," she said, rolling

up the washed greens and then cutting them the way both her mother and her great-grandmother had taught her.

"Do I get to meet your little boyfriend today?" Mama Belle teased.

Dionne shook her head. She hadn't seen Hassan since the move although they talked, texted, Twittered and were on Facebook all the time. When she'd invited him for Thanksgiving dinner, he'd said his parents wanted to spend the day with him and Dionne's spirits had just plummeted.

"Not sure if you're old enough for a boyfriend," Ma Belle said as she poured lemon over her pound cake.

"He's a nice boy from the old neighborhood," Risha said, giving Dionne a wink. "I know his parents, he's on the football team, and he gets good grades in school."

Dionne smiled with pride. Hassan was a cool boyfriend. Not a bit of thug in him, although he wasn't a punk.

"Humph, I hope y'all talk about sex or the lack of it," Mama Belle stressed.

Dionne flushed in embarrassment. "Mama Belle."

"Yes, we have and I told her more than once to keep her panties up and her skirt down and she'd be okay," Risha joked.

Mama Belle huffed. "Truer words have never been spoken."

"Yes, ma'am," Risha said, deferring to her elder.

"All little boys want one thing from little girls," Mama Belle said.

"It must be conversation, because that's all I'm offering," Dionne said truthfully.

Mama Belle just sucked air between her teeth.

"There's Keke Palmer," Dionne said, using the remote to turn the volume up on the television and hopefully changing the subject.

"Ooh, her outfit is cute," Risha said, helping Dionne change the subject.

Dionne nodded. She loved, loved, loved Keke Palmer since *Akeelah and the Bee.* "Love the black sequined pants with the purple wool trench."

"Humph," Mama Belle grunted.

Dionne and Risha just shared a look before they both stopped what they were doing and put Mama Belle in the middle of a love sandwich as they hugged her tight and pressed kisses to her cheek.

That turned her frown into a smile.

Hours later, Dionne came running down the stairs as soon as she heard the doorbell ring. She smoothed her off-the-shoulder sweater dress with a big bulky belt as she pulled the door open wide. Her dad carried two big bags but Dionne weighed his neck down as she hugged him real close—especially when she didn't see Candylixxxious with him. "Happy Thanksgiving, Daddy," she said, grinning like a fool as she left a big gooey lip-gloss smear on his cheek.

"Whaddup, baby girl," he said, looking real nice in his suede blazer, V-neck sweater and jeans.

"Where's Grandma Les?" she asked.

He shook his head and laughed, his grill shining. "She ain't ready to be messed with again."

Dionne was hurt. "She'd rather choose hating Mama

than seeing me?" she asked. "I'm her only grand…far as I know."

Lahron lifted his shades to eye her. "Don't play with me and how 'bout next weekend me and you both go spend it with her. How 'bout dat?"

Dionne's first thought was "Bump her," but she just nodded, remembering to always have respect.

"You all preppy," she said, stepping back from him.

"Trying to dress it up a little bit for the holidays and the new house," he said, looking around as he stepped inside the foyer.

"Daddy, please don't argue with Mama. Not today," she pleaded, only half playing.

He laughed. "I got you. I got you."

She pushed the door closed and moved to follow him into the den where a football game was on the flat screen.

"Can I come in?"

Dionne froze and whirled around to see Hassan standing in the doorway with a huge bouquet of flowers in his hands. She smiled as she felt herself go weak as she rushed to him and pushed him back out the door to reach up and grab his face. "Has," she breathed.

"You surprised?" he asked, his cologne surrounding her along with the cold winds. "Your dad picked me up and—"

Dionne got on her tiptoes and pressed her mouth to his, enjoying having him near her again.

Hassan brought his hands up to lightly touch Dionne's hips, the tips of the flowers brushing against the ends of her hair.

Chills...up and down my spine.

"Humph."

Dionne whirled to find Mama Belle standing in the doorway eyeing them. She motioned for them to come inside and mumbled something about throwing cold water on them.

Dionne and Hassan both tried to hide their smiles as they walked into the house.

thirty-two

Marisol
November 26@2:00 p.m. | Mood: Grateful (& Relieved)

"YOU got the part!"

Marisol smiled any time she thought about Eli screaming like a fool in her ear last night when he called her with the good news. "Now I just have to convince Mami and Papi."

She knew that was going to be an uphill battle. They supported her love of dance, but their focus for her was—and always would be—education, education, education.

As she stepped out of her bathroom in her white terrycloth robe, fresh from a shower, Marisol remembered how alive she'd felt during the audition, even though the dance studio had been filled with more than a hundred other dancers besides her. Eli and his partner had given them all intricate dance routines to learn in the blink of the eye and Marisol had never failed. Soon those who made the cut had dwindled and dwindled until there were ten, and then five, and then three.

And she got the part.

She danced around in her robe, throwing it up into the air to float above her for a second as she spun around.

She hadn't told a soul yet. But she knew because of her age she had to get her parents' approval. If not, whoever came in second would be in the video by default.

"Liar, liar, pants on fire..."

Marisol eyed her cell phone as the childish rant sounded in the air. The days of "there goes my baby" were long gone for Percy. Long gone.

She was sick of his excuses and not willing to listen to them. Marisol was determined not to be that chick who let a man run over her, lie to her, cheat on her and disrespect her. Nope, not gonna happen.

She massaged her body with lotion and pulled her curls back into a tight ponytail before she dressed in jeans and a T-shirt, definitely against her forever-be-fabulous rule.

The task at hand was more important than wearing a thousand-dollar outfit. After pulling on a pair of loafers, she grabbed her big tote and left her room.

It was hard not to be taken in by the smells wafting through the house. The kitchen was alive with food and the usual smells of Thanksgiving dinner being prepared. Both her father's and mother's sides of the family always gathered at their home for huge family gatherings.

Marisol's mouth watered at the thought of all the traditional Spanish foods—ham, cheese, chorizo sausage, shepherd soup, seafood pasta salads, roasted pigs, lamb, rice, vegetables and a mixed green salad. And the desserts? Marisol sighed. For days after the holiday, the family would eat *abuela's mantecados* (crumb cake), *turrons* (almond candies) and *polvorones* (almond cookies).

Muy delicioso!

Marisol knocked on Carlos's door. "Let's go, Booger," she loudly called to him outside his bedroom door.

Moments later it opened. A disgruntled and pouting Carlos stepped out into the hall as the sounds of family reached them from below. "I don't see why I have to go," he said, clearly not in a good mood.

"Because we're all going, so get over it," she told him, tugging on the bill of his ever-present baseball cap.

She frowned when she thought she'd heard him curse. She gave him a hard look as if she was his mother and not just his older sister.

"Sorry," he muttered, shoving his hands into the pockets of his cargo khakis as they descended the stairs.

Soon she would have another little brother or sister to keep in line as the oldest of the Rivera children. And the baby was really taking their mother through her paces.

Just a warning of what's to come, Marisol thought as her mother and father stepped into the foyer, both dressed in jeans and sweaters.

"Sí," Marisol and her brother answered.

"Mami, we'll be back in a couple of hours," Alex said in Spanish as he helped his wife into her coat.

Marisol was the first out the door, ready for Thanksgiving. The food and the family were great, but this day for her was all about showing just how thankful she was for a really good life.

Because of the holidays, the Rivera household staff was

off and so Alex had to park his own Land Rover in front of the mansion. He helped his wife into the passenger seat and their children climbed into the back.

"Daddy, do you remember the video I told you about?" she asked in rapid Spanish.

He eyed her in the rearview mirror. "No, Marisol."

"But I auditioned with, like, a hundred girls and I got the part," she said, proud of herself.

Yasmine turned in her seat to eye her. "You did?" she gasped in surprise.

"Must've not been much competition," Carlos mumbled.

Marisol pinched his thigh.

"Ow!" he cried.

"Marisol!" her father snapped.

"Sorry," she mumbled.

Yasmine was the one to give Carlos a disapproving look for his smart comment. She smiled when she focused on Marisol. "We need more information, and then your father and I will talk it over and get back to you."

"Yasmine," he said in warning.

Marisol watched as her mother reached her hand out to massage the back of her father's neck.

"I only said we would get more information and talk about it," she said softly to him in Spanish. Very softly.

Marisol saw her father's shoulders relax a bit. That was just as good as a yes.

She danced on the inside. *Yahoooo!* she thought.

During their ride, she texted Starr, Dionne and Natalee to check in on everyone's holiday.

When she told them her plans for the day, Dionne commended her, Natalee admired her and Starr didn't understand her—at all.

Her friends made her smile. Starr was adjusting to Natalee being in their clique. Not adjusting well, but adjusting nonetheless. Natalee was just too fabulous for Starr to take at times. Effortlessly fabulous, which made it all the worse for Starr.

Thankfully the buzz about Natalee's performance during the talent show was dying down. Marisol giggled at how red Starr's face would get anytime someone gushed over Natalee in front of her.

"Seriously, what would you do if you saw Jesus?" she had snapped once.

Starr was such a diva.

Marisol shook her head as she remembered a surprise she had planned for Starr. In the days after her breakup with Percy, she had forgotten all about it. Nice little surprise for Thanksgiving, she thought.

"Where in the hello and goodbye are we?" Carlos roared loudly.

"Carlos!" both of her parents yelled.

Marisol eyed him, knowing he had gotten the play on words from her. The little monster had to be eavesdropping on her conversations.

She finally looked out the window and even though she was more prepared than her little brother, the sight of the line of people outside still made her nervous.

"A quien mucho se da, mucho se espera… A quien mucho se da, mucho se espera," Marisol repeated over and over as a

police officer and her parents' publicist, Sandy, waved him through the open gates of the parking lot.

"To whom much is given, much is expected," Marisol repeated the quote in English.

She was just glad they were mindful enough to not show up at a homeless shelter in a five-thousand-dollar outfit. That woulda been *soooo* wrong on *soooo* many levels.

Serving food to the homeless on Thanksgiving was Marisol's idea. She was determined to use her father's fame to do good things. As soon as they walked into the building, Marisol reached in her tote bag for the envelope. There were media people present and other local celebrities participating in the event. Her parents' publicist stepped forward to introduce them to the executive director of the shelter.

"I have a donation for your shelter," Marisol said as the woman shook her hand.

Sandy stepped forward, her smile white and brilliant against her smooth dark complexion. "A what?" she asked.

It wasn't about publicity. She focused her attention on the executive director. "My friends and I won a five-hundred-dollar prize at our school talent show. We're donating it to your shelter," she said, pressing it into the woman's hand.

Sandy looked back and snapped her finger. "Get me one of the news reporters," she said sharply before reaching out to pull the envelope out of the woman's grasp. "We'll get the donation on camera, if that's okay."

Marisol frowned and quickly took the envelope back from Sandy and pressed it back into the executive director's hand. "It's not for publicity," she said.

The executive director, a tall, broad woman with kind eyes and salt-and-pepper dreadlocks down her back, smiled and reached down to hug Marisol close. "You have a good spirit, child. God bless you," she said softly.

Marisol was determined to see fame put to use for good.

And now that I learned the lesson, I won't ever forget it.

thirty-three

Starr

November 26@3:00 p.m. | Mood: Blessed

starr wandered around the massive great room with a small glass of warm apple cider. Nearly fifty or so people mingled about the areas of the space. Most were family, some were close friends, and some business associates. Nearly all of the TopStarr artists and their family were attending the Lester Thanksgiving of catered food from Butterfield's.

Except for Jordan.

Starr had to admit that it would have been nice to chill with him, but his family had traveled to Georgia for the holidays. She reached into the pocket of her BCBG, dark chocolate, strapless dress for her iPhone as she walked into the foyer and sat down on the stairs. She dialed Jordan's number.

"Excuse me."

Starr was looking down. Her eyes shifted to the black Jordans in front of her feet and up the long legs and slender body to the face of the cutie smiling down at her.

"Hel—"

Starr ended the call even as Jordan said hello. "Hi, can I help you?" she asked, already rising to her feet.

In her heels the top of her head came just below his chin. The dark brown shirt he wore under a chocolate racing jacket perfectly matched her outfit. His cologne didn't overpower her perfume.

Perfect height, she thought. Good style. She could do without the braids but this dude was a definite cutie—a younger version of that male model Keston Karter. He would easily make Top 5 of their Hot Boyz list.

"I'm looking for my sister Angie," he said, his voice deep.

Her phone rang and she sent it to voice mail.

"Angie's right inside," she said, pointing toward the entryway to the great room.

"Thanks," he said, moving past her.

Starr's eyes followed him as he walked away with his bowlegged swagger, which kicked him up at least a notch or two or three. (Jordan was always her number one.)

Her phone vibrated in her hand. "Hey, Jordan," she said, standing up to walk over to the entryway of the great room. Her eyes sought and found *The Cutie.* He was standing by his sister Angie by the fireplace.

"Miss me, huh?" Jordan asked.

The Cutie looked up and caught Starr looking at him.

She quickly turned her back to him as her heart pounded like crazy.

"Starr?"

She shook her head to clear it. "Huh?"

"Miss me?" Jordan said again.

I was until…

"Excuse me again."

Starr froze and sent her eyes heavenward, before she made her face blank and turned around to face the guy that could be her newest crush. "I'll call you back," she said, ending the call with a press of her short neatly trimmed thumb.

Jordan? Forgotten, at least for now.

"Your dad asked for you," he said, his voice so smooth.

"Okay." Starr gave him her most flirty smile. *I'm available—not desperate. Interested—but not stalker-ish.*

They walked into the room together.

"What's your name?" she asked, ignoring her vibrating phone as she slid it back into the pocket of her skirt.

"Karl with a *K,*" he said, extending his hand to her as they walked across the room.

"Nice jacket, Karl with a *K,*" she said, flirting hard. "I'm Starr."

"I know," he said, before easing away to reclaim his spot next to his sister.

Starr forced herself not to sneak another peek at him as

she came to stand in front of her father. She smiled politely at the man he was speaking to.

"Excuse me," her father said, reaching out to place her hand around his arm.

"Attention, everyone. Attention," Cole Lester yelled out.

Starr looked around at everyone, thoroughly confused. Her mother looked up from wiping one of the twins' mouth and gave her a reassuring smile.

"Just wanted to welcome a new member to the TopStarr Records family," Cole said, as the maids began to hand everyone twenty-one and older a glass of champagne. Underage guests received glasses of sparkling cider.

Starr accepted her flute.

"Everyone raise your glass to congratulate my daughter for helping me discover a dope producer out of Atlanta and for selling her first song to TopStarr Productions," he said.

Starr's eyes popped wide-open. "Really, Daddy?" she asked.

He nodded before taking a deep sip of his champagne as the room burst into applause and some whistles.

Starr hugged his neck, still careful not to spill anything on their clothes.

"How much money am I making?" she asked.

Everyone laughed.

Starr frowned. "No, I'm serious," she continued.

Everyone laughed harder.

"That's my daughter," Cole joked.

But I'm serious, she thought as everyone came forward to congratulate her.

Later that night, stuffed from all of the food, Starr was lounging around her room weighing her old crush on Jordan and her newfound one for Karl. She definitely was going to find out more about Karl. The essentials: age, relationship status, car status, future goals. She'd definitely felt a vibe that he was interested, especially when he'd made sure to sit next to her during dinner.

It was one of the most nerve-racking meals as she tried to stay cute while eating Thanksgiving dinner.

She opened the file on her laptop for the Hot Boyz list. *Time for a new entry,* she thought.

Name:	Karl Hunter
Age:	18
B-Day:	TBA (To Be Asked)
Fab Cred:	So far completely all about the swag.
Cute Factor:	10!!! (Keston Karter look-alike? Def a 10. Helloooo.)
Style Factor:	TBD (To Be Determined) becuz one

outfit is not enough to decide style.
:(

Hot Boyz Rank: Not a Pace student but def Top 5!!!

Starr quickly uploaded the picture she'd sneaked of him with her camera phone and added it to his file. She had so much to fill all the girls in on: her possible new crush and her and Fiyah selling the song she wrote to his track. Life was pretty good even out of the spotlight. Songwriters made all the real money anyway, with less sweat than performers.

There was definitely more than one way to make a name for herself and claim fame in her own right. She couldn't sing a lick but she could write songs that other people could. She liked the sound of that.

Starr had even readjusted to the uniform policy at school. If anyone wondered why she took it in stride, they never asked, and she wasn't offering up the goods. No need for them to know that having to wear uniforms had quashed any chance of Natalee wearing some to-die-for Gucci ensemble at Pace Academy. Suddenly blending in wasn't such a bad thing.

She gave Karl the Cutie's picture one last once-over before she saved and then closed the file. She checked her email. She was surprised to see something from Marisol. There was a video attached.

Maybe it was of their performance at the talent show? she wondered, as she downloaded the attachment.

"But how would she get it before me?" Starr asked herself aloud. She was the one who had hired the video crew to record their performance.

The video opened on her laptop screen. Starr adjusted the lighting so that everything didn't look so dark. She frowned at the sight of a door opening and then a tall, dark-haired woman in a red dress walking into a bathroom stall and closing the door behind her. The camera turned and suddenly Marisol's face filled the screen.

"You will not believe who just walked into that stall," Marisol said in a loud whisper.

"Who is that out there?" the voice from the stall said.

Starr gasped in surprise. Kimora!

Marisol giggled and winked at the camera. "Um, hello, Miss Kimora. This is Marisol Rivera, Alex Rivera's daughter," she said loudly, bouncing up and down.

The commode flushed.

"Um, when you're done, would you mind sending a video message to my friend Starr?" she asked. "Pleeeeeaaaassse."

Starr was tense like she was watching a real movie. Her palms were sweaty and her heart raced as she clutched her rhinestone mouse like her life depended on it.

The camera turned back around as the bathroom stall

opened and the Fabulous One walked out, all tall, curvy, famous and fabulous.

"Hi, Starr," said Kimora. "Your friend is crazy, but remember to always stay fabulous!" She blew a kiss at the screen just before the camera went black.

★ ★ ★ ★ ★

Discussion Questions

1) Starr is proud of her parents' success and enjoys the fruits of their labor. But if you were Starr would you want to have your own claim to fame? And would you choose to do something you loved over something that would make you rich? Why?

2) Dionne is still learning to deal with her father's new-found fame and was excited about her own chance to shine as a Go Getta. Do you think she values her father's advice over her mother's? Do you think it was appropriate for her to live in the master bedroom suite of their new house? If you were in her shoes, what would you have done?

3) Fame is not as important to Marisol as her love and passion for dancing. She would dance for a living—even if it meant struggling financially. Is there something you are passionate about, regardless of whether you become famous or not? What steps are you taking—or should you be taking—to have the career of your dreams?

4) Marisol brought cultural diversity to the clique (and

a lot of Latina flare). What do you all think about the addition of Natalee to the clique?

5) Starr truly believed that she was going to sing her way to fame. Her friends didn't have the heart to tell her that she was tone-deaf. If you were Starr, would you want your friends to be honest with you…even if it hurt your feelings?

6) Marisol learned that fame can have a positive side, too, like the charity work her mother does. If you were famous, would you use your celebrity for good to help the less fortunate or would you just enjoy the good life?

7) Natalee was being home-schooled but really felt like she was missing out on the fun of going to school. If you had the opportunity to be home-schooled, would you? What would you miss about school?

8) Starr is pretty strong-willed and usually gets what she wants, when she wants it. Her heart wants Jordan, but her mind tells her that he wants a relationship that's more than she's ready for. Since she is such a strong person, couldn't she just resist temptation? Do you think Starr made the right decision to just remain friends with Jordan?

9) Dionne continues to struggle trying to balance both her worlds, but she finally decided that she likes Hassan.

Should Dionne trust that her friends will accept Hassan or do you understand her hesitation?

10) All three of the girls wanted to form the group and try for fame without their parents' help. If you were one of the Pacesetters with rich and famous parents, would you want their help? Yes? No? And why or why not?

Author's Note

Hello again, everyone,

Two down and more to go in the Pace Academy series. I thank you for purchasing *FAMOUS*. You've learned a little more about the fabulous Pacesetters clique and the exclusive private school Pace Academy in Saddle River, New Jersey.

I cannot express my gratitude for all the love and support that readers have shown for this series. Thank you for understanding that, like anything else in this world, fiction needs balance. Some books are serious, some books are literary, some magical...and some just plain fun. That's where this series comes in. I just want you to have fun while reading. To dream a little. To be fabulous and famous in your own world. It's possible. Believe me.

The girls learn the high price of fame, and survive it with help from each other. That's what friends do. But there are more lessons to be learned and more fun to be had. In book three, the Pacesetters discover just what it takes to be glamorous and decide if it's really worth it. The drama continues...big-time. LOL.

Stay tuned for more details and be sure to spread the word that the Pacesetters are here!

Best,
Simone
xoxo

About the Author

FAMOUS is Simone Bryant's second work of young adult fiction in the Pace Academy series, centered around the Pacesetters clique. Simone Bryant is the pseudonym for Niobia Bryant, a national bestselling author of romance fiction, mainstream fiction and urban fiction.

For more on the Pacesetters series and its author, please visit:
MySpace: www.myspace.com/beapacesetter
Twitter: www.twitter.com/beapacesetter
Facebook: Search: Simone Bryant—Teen Fiction Author
Shelfari: www.shelfari.com/unlimited_ink

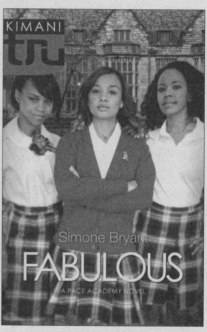